Stark Raving Blue

The Cheap Stories compendium

Richard Weems

WbW Ink   New Jersey

Printed in the United States of America

Cover design by Richard Weems

ISBN: 0-9974332-0-5
ISBN-13: 978-0-9974332-0-3

WbW Ink
28 Rockridge Rd.
Haskell, NJ

www.facebook.com/CheapStories

This is a work of fiction. Names, characters, places, and incidents either are the products of the author's imagination or are used fictitiously. Any resemblance to actual persons, living or dead, businesses, companies, events, or locales is entirely coincidental.

For Svea, my BabyMine.

CONTENTS

ESSAYS

ACKNOWLEDGMENTS

The works contained in this compendium were previously released in Kindle-only chapbooks, the Cheap Stories Series

Thanks go out to the following magazines, who originally published previous versions of these works:

Pif Magazine - "The Need for Character," "Self-Interview," "Mercy," "Falling," "Democritus' Atom," "Poor Tree," "The Way of It," "Writing the Blue Book," "Violence," "Rules of Combat" and "Dangerous Theatre"

New World Writing - "After Art," "Paradigms," "The Book of Roger" and "Soup"

Story Bytes - "The Cat Strangler," "No More, No More" and "Padre"

Melic Review - "Together, the Choir Grows Old"

Crescent Review - "The Fine Art of Fletcherism"

Sparks - "Apples"

La Petite Zine - "Textual Notes to a Lost Work"

Barcelona Review - "Curbsides Boxes"

InterText - "The Smart Bomb"

Brick Street - "Tell Everything"

Weirderary - "Forecast"

Air in the Paragraph Line - "Sitting Danny Rolling"

NOTE: The original Cheap Stories series also included an imbedded link that opened to an original video, "The Dream of Pigs: A Memory."

For obvious reasons, an imbedded link will not work in a printed format.

To see the video, please go to YouTube and search for "The Dream of Pigs: A Memory."

Introduction

Weems and I finally met in 2001 at a Melt-Banana show in NYC's former Knitting Factory. He was barely 30 years old. Old enough to have written a bit of fiction, just old enough to have finished his MFA. As the Editor of *Pif Magazine*, I had published several of his stories. They were so terrifyingly good that I insisted on meeting him. His hair was dyed Kool-Aid red. He had the ease of a big guy who had spent years working the doors of East Village clubs. He upped the ante all night with his humorous admirations for Padgett Powell, Harry Crews, and other faculty we had each gone out drinking with at one point or another. Weems lobbed serious fiction at me too—"Which Borges have you read?" "What about Joy Williams? Isn't she hiding in the Keys now?" "Lish utterly changed the way I approach a sentence, cranky fuck that he is."

Our talking points weren't that different twelve years later. Melt-Banana played this time at an old Greenpoint bar in the fall of 2013, and we found symmetry in making this our next meeting.

But Weems was changed. The emergence of Fast Fiction had intensified his already condensed phrasing. He had gained a trusted rhythm with the independent magazine editors who he wanted to impress. He had written so many good and nuanced stories. His hair was not red.

He talked about his own students now. The immensely talented ones he was committed to help. The ones who blistered his ideas about how to write.

He discussed with responsibility what little new writing there was to be passionate about. The faculty we had discussed a dozen years earlier were 40-plus when they first wrote with sustained impact. "We're that age now," he pointed out. Japanese noise rock ensued around us.

I came home and reread *Anything He Wants*, "The Need for Character," "Writing the Blue Book," and other Weems stories. His first sentences wooed me. I cried when the Bunny left the bar. Ancient literature—fables, parables, and hymns—contained the same compressed conflicts of event and language.

Fifteen years after first publishing Weems, I am pleased to introduce his compendium. Weems has always seen his mission as sharing the contemporary plight of the confused, sad, and inspired masses, and his characters are more like us now than ever. Over and again, the rush of conversation coupled with a galvanizing narrative exceed his wise aim. These stories exhibit the enormous range of a great writing talent and his particularly wry version of modern humanity.

You must read this book.

—Camille Renshaw

FICTION

The Need for Character

The virtue of hope, in Enoch, was made of two
parts suspicion and one part lust...He wanted,
some day, to see a line of people waiting to shake
his hand.
—Flannery O'Connor,
"Enoch and the Gorilla"

Until this morning, my story was the same any other yokel
leaning on the brass rail at 9 a.m. could tell you. Until this
morning, there was no reason to tell my story to anyone but
the tenderer of the booze and every-goddamn-one else like
me: hiding in the dark in broad daylight, feeling safe with
those who suffered alike and also knew a kind of safety in
anonymity.

But this Bunny sitting next to me had ears and great rayon
paws that folded all the way around his rocks glass. He
beamed pink in this place that had not seen such color in a
long, long time. He had a tail that exploded from his ass like
nuclear activity. This Bunny had a genuine beef to make and
a pile of money, and he was buying for me as long as I was
listening. His face was beet red even through the white and
pink make-up, and it got redder still with each double splash
of Wild Turkey straight up, his grease paint whiskers getting
more and more ethereal by the minute. Graying human
whiskers peeked out from beneath.

"Damn them," the Bunny screamed, "and their parents too, unable to teach them a thing or two about toilet training."

Back we were to the kids climbing onto his lap, their seats wet with unbridled excitement.

"All I'm supposed to do," the Bunny said, looking at me over his empty granny glass frames, "is smile and wave and tell them, 'What good little children, oh what happy and good little boys and girls we have here.' Pah!" His face pulled in around his constricted mouth. "A pox! A hail of brimstone and kitty litter upon their heads! *I'm* the one who has to go home with myself after letting these kids climb all over my lap. You should see how my legs smell at the end of a day. The bastards!"

The Bunny slapped the bar with his pink, heavy paw, this time harder. A glass shook somewhere out there amongst the others, hard to see them in this artificial dark. The Bunny's ears flopped with the effort.

What I admired most in this Bunny was his courage to stand out. In a crowded mall, kids could see him from a hundred yards off. These kids probably came screaming at him. All this character, all this distinction and unique quality, and these kids with their puddled pants didn't even know his name.

"'Mr. Bunny, Mr. Bunny,' they call me" (his ears waved in a fury now, bending against the rigidity of their wire frames). He threw back another hit, motioned to his pile of money for more. "What do they care? My name could be Henry. My name could be Oscar, Mersault, Bradley. My name could even be goddamn Jill. Who cares? They don't goddamn know it, and I don't goddamn know it, but how am I supposed to goddamn know it? All I get is a suit. I get a chart on how to paint my face. I'm told to call them good little girls and boys and put them on my lap and smile and take a few pictures. No script, no motivation, no context on the nature of being the Easter Bunny in today's society, nothing."

Shining through was the thespian in him, the need for soul, a part with history and needs and wants and desires and subtext. I was agreeing with this man, this Bunny, because he was the one with the money and I had a tab that could make the strongest man wince—but still, it was obvious. Even I could have been the Bunny if the need for character was all it took.

"I could be a Nathan," the Bunny continued, "a Ross. I could be Jonathan Nathaniel Zimmerman, I could be Edwin Arlington Robinson even, for all those fuckers care." He looked at the clock. It was ten minutes until the mall opened.

"Oh, jeez." The Bunny slid from his stool, and his large feet made nary a sound as they met the floor. The Bunny was on his way out, the remnants of his money clutched in a paw.

What I'm trying to tell you is this: in that instant I knew it:

I could have been the Bunny. The suit was big enough to fit anyone.

I could have been the Bunny. I'd know my name.

"Hold up, hold up," I called, but he was nearly out the door already. I left behind my drink and charged out after his rolling, exaggerated hips. I could have grabbed him right there, by the puff of his tail maybe. It was a good chance to catch him unawares and give me the element of surprise and the first swing at him, but I had to wait until we were out of sight of the others (I didn't want them to think the Bunny and me were lovers or anything like that) who were still hiding in the dark and were never going to get the chance to find their names this easily and weren't going to find their names in a long, long time.

After Art

Still, every now and then, you get guys in here asking for Art. I tell them, "No. No Art tonight," because that's the truth of the matter, and then these guys will turn right around and go back the way they came, their heads bowed sometimes but always shaking. They leave like they're leaving a funeral. And they are, really—even the regulars don't come around anymore.

When we had Art, there was no room here for anything else. If you're tired of standing around, the rumor went, just pick your feet up. They stood in line out the door, around the parking lot and back. They got food at the Starvin' Marvin's down the road and had picnics in the street, they had to wait so long. All just to take hold of the harness strapped to Art's back and have their turn flinging that damn midget as far as they could. We had waitresses too, the biggest waitresses we could find—six-foot-one the shortest of them. They broke up fights when the bouncers had trouble getting through the crowd, and they had free reign to clock any wise-ass copping a feel. It was easy to scam drinks, then, for then it was too busy for anyone to check up on you—a push here, a slide on the other end. A good bartender could clear a couple bills before he even started emptying his jar.

Now there's supposed to be room in back for a kitchen, a deli, maybe, somewhere to make sandwiches, but these new owners don't know a thing about running a place like this. The old guy, Sam, sold out long ago. His wife and two daughters left him soon after Art, like they knew things were only going to pot, and Sam, he cracked—put every bit of his money into land, and bought up a long tract outside Palatka. I heard he tried bringing his wife back by promising to build a house, but there's no money to build a house. All he has is land, and he likes to sit back and admire the view. I hear he's put up a roof, perched on the ends of two-by-four's, and there he's got a cot, a 12-gauge with no ammunition, a tool chest, a rocking chair with a cracked runner, his Rottweiller, Kirkegaard (the dog came with that name), matches, lantern, a Coleman cooler and a sink that isn't connected. I hear he spends his days playing fetch with Kirkegaard, and before throwing out that stick, I hear he looks off into the untamed woods that is his land and thinks of when the dance floor was nothing but a sea of heads topped with waitresses like foam riding over wakes, like mermaids, the people brimming and sweating and clenching their fists, all wanting to get their hands on Art, who waited for them in his bright yellow jumpsuit, grinning as if he couldn't wait to be thrown again...

But you should have seen that little guy fly through the air —turning, I tell you, turning in the air, spinning around like a bagel, like a goddamn egg bagel on the wing. And everyone wanted a piece of him.

Paradigms

It all started quietly: Regional Manager Vincent Johnson paged Mutzweiller in Advertising to see if the man wouldn't mind showing up for his own presentation. One secretary—flustered, stalling—covered the receiver incompletely and whispered to another, "Go see if Mr. Mutzweiller's back yet."

"Back?" the other asked.

"If he's..." a bit hushed, though still audible between her fingers, "zoomed. You know, back." A sound—a quick gesture involving the arm and wrist.

Footsteps headed away, a door opened, then the hold music.

Then through the grapevine, a tale of Thracken in Contracts's team running themselves unruly while a client large in economics and body type boomed complaints in the waiting room regarding his precious time. Thracken on line one, collect from Istanbul (Istanbul?), the secretaries calling Research, asking what might lure a pig out from under some brush.

No one has pointed any fingers, but wherever it started, however long it took, most all the execs at the Eastern Branch Office are trying it. Setting up pup tents in their offices, squeezing into them holding potbelly pigs, and with a ping! or pop! (or zoom!), they're teleporting out to foreign lands, seeing sights, sampling the local fare, buying Asian prostitutes (male and female), and not getting back for scheduled appointments, synergistic trainings, face-time with supervisors.

"It's the damn pigs," Corkle, Johnson's snitch, confides.

"Soon as they teleport, these pigs get ornery, damn hard to hold, and they take off. Seems you can only get back with the same pig you rode out with." Corkle is up to putting his feet on Johnson's desk. A steady progression—rigid and formal at first, nervous to be the company spy, then relaxed and willing to accept a bourbon, then slouched and comfortable that his secret goes both ways, then his feet up on Johnson's desk. Regional Manager Johnson can't recall the first time it happened. Seems like Corkle had his feet on the desk a long time before they actually got up there.

"These pigs wriggle away quickly, leave you beating shrubbery. Olman in Graphics keeps his on a leash, but that only gets him as far as Florida, once to the Haitian Islands. A free-range pig will take you anywhere you please." Corkle is fresh from business school in Wyoming, a descendant of pig farmers. He believes in the old school of getting ahead: get an in with the boss. No win-win attitude, interdependency, seeking first to understand before being understood. Corkle wants the bigger office and a team of private secretaries, the best accommodations for conventions, he wants them now, and that means ratting on anything Johnson wants to know about.

"Already, if you can't get out of the hemisphere, you have nothing to say at the water cooler."

As yet, the Home Office in Texas hasn't deemed this situation a big enough problem to take out of Johnson's hands (or maybe because they don't want to spread word that execs from all over the country might be chasing pigs through foreign streets), and Johnson's efforts have nary made a dent. Endless memos only challenge the printing budget and show commission signs in the eyes of copier repairmen. The guards at sign-in have instructions to check all gym bags, not allow in tent boxes, listen for muffled grunts, but the problems go on just the same. Corkle has even gotten wind of a pig pusher—someone in Budgeting, possibly, skulking swine through hallways (under coats? buried under envelopes in mailbins?). Spot checks have revealed tents hastily stowed in broom closets and drop ceilings, a pig in a cat caddie hidden under a planter stand, maps of China and Thailand with circles around cities and sites, some checked off, some not. The checks have ranks of 1 to 10.

"Thailand is a favorite," Corkle reveals.

There is a secret newsletter circulating. Tips, helpful articles on how much casual wear will fit inside a briefcase, reader mail, all in code names: Leonard C., Maury A., Gwynivere S. Corkle provides Johnson with a regular subscription, but the names mystify them both. The initials Johnson could have figured out on his own—department. There's no Gwynivere in Sales, but Corkle has divined possibilities from anagrams, known reading habits, mathematical theorem (the number of letters in the code name corresponding to the perpetrator's executive floor), offered to Johnson in the most professional presentation Johnson has seen since before Mutzweiller's first disappearance. But Corkle can offer only hypotheses—word's out there's a snitch, so people aren't talking much.

Other signs of things getting worse: Ellenberry, VP of Marketing, out on leave due to a bad fall in the Antarctic, his life saved only because the pig was too cold to abandon the confines of Ellenberry's oversized coat; a cursory check of the mailroom reveals a community tent, a pig with a company name tag, "Buster"; the executive floors teem with absentia during the lunch hour.

"Someone started a pool for most dangerous transport," Corkle reports. "They gather in one of the lounges, watch CNN and dare each other to get as close as possible to a California brush fire, an earthquake in Chile, the running of the bulls." Corkle shows no concern at all about his feet. It's as if he has them on his own desk. He hardly pays attention to Johnson's probing questions anymore. He has the stare now—of reminiscence, of sights seen.

Johnson backed into a corner. The items he confiscated have to be returned. Tents reclaimed from custodial storage, company checks issued for pig replacement.

"Teleportational harassment," the letter, championed by official-sounding names (Jewish, mostly), threatens. Everyone is permitted a lunch hour and two twenty-minute breaks, and since the average teleportation uses only 91.47 minutes of company time (no citation for this figure), there are no grounds for threats or termination. Unfortunate incidents where teleportation impeded company operations cannot be a basis for disciplinary action—this mode of transportation can be executed on company property and therefore provides undue strain to its workers, who are being given no instruction or otherwise appropriate consideration on how to control and contain this temptation. A ruling is cited, where management of a meat-packing plant was not legally justified in terminating any meat packer (packed into what? boxes? cans? paper? plastic?) for use of the hallucinogenic fungi that grew in abundance in the plant's back lot for the same reasons. Besides, the unusual nature of these teleportations, their ease and immediacy, leaves no distinction between a visit to New Zealand and a quick run down to the corner Pizzeria Uno. A quick trip to Bali constitutes no more a threat to company business than a cigarette break, and is the pressure on these employees as discriminatory as delving into employees' personal lives, or holding it against a female when she gets pregnant?

Johnson trifles, yells at his secretaries for no reason, chain-smokes in non-smoking areas. Texas is finally offering 'solutions': company communiqués filled with suggestions from world-famous chefs on the best spots for lunch, what places are willing to offer a pig check. A new personnel manual: *Sow-Handling: How to Care for Your Tele-Buddy*. A complimentary leash wall by each restroom; safety training and supervised field trips; a pigpen next to daycare. Ideas offered up by thinkers and P.R. experts and lawyers behind desks and in tanks filled with others of their own kind.

Johnson spends hours looking for dents in his desk from Corkle's heel. He feels his authority leaking from him by the bucketful. Once upon a time, the lower execs cleared the way at board meetings when he decided to sit next to Price in Sales's secretary, the minutes-taker—tall and auburn and just the slightest hint of perfume, slightest hint of baby powder, slightest hint of breast under conservative blouses, the kind that will take you on your desk (everyone knows that), pant like a dog in your ear. When he drew close, she would straighten her posture, subtly but noticeably, and lick her lips. How can Johnson explain that no one moves aside for him anymore? That there is no one left to move? That Corkle visits without an appointment now, his feet instantaneously on Johnson's desk, his pup tent steaming from a fresh teleport, Johnson's staff off in Bangkok, Bangladesh, Burma?

Every now and then, Corkle removes his shoes.

Every now and then, Johnson believes himself transported to a strange place: purple trees, pink kiwi fruit running in parabola-shaped flocks, garbage cans just starting to blossom. Johnson reeking of pig slop, his little potbelly, Edgar, gone off forever, leaving Johnson alone with nothing but his pup tent and his wits (then again, his pup tent)...and then he thrusts awake, panting, palpitating, sun beaming between the vertical blinds of his high-rise condo, burning right into his brain.

Johnson tries all the quick-fix methods: primal scream, stress balls, aromatherapy. He calls the company help line, but the anonymous voice on the other end can't make him out. Pigs? Saigon? The auburn secretary? Johnson—unshaven, shirts wrinkled and loose, suspenders not connected in the back—lets his habit of coming in drunk worsen. His office is littered with the clanking of bottles Johnson doesn't bother to clean up anymore. The industrial supply of Wrigley's Spearmint in his desk drawer untouched, for there is no one left to hide from, the executive floors quiet as a mausoleum except when the central air kicks in, or when the phones ring, but these aren't business calls anymore. Clients are being given international numbers, agendas for what countries can be reached on what days. The only incoming calls are voice mails. Every now and then, Johnson picks up a receiver and pretends to be voice mail.

"Hey Morgan, your Tuvan romp is the best." The phone is held up to the sound of inhuman voices, chanting as though through a life of too many cigarettes. "I made it to Kyzyl, man. I'm taking throat-singing lessons. I'm going to milk a yak."

Johnson dances through the vacant corridors, exposes himself to empty desks, laughs until he coughs and spits. He's stopped wearing pants. He expects to see wisps of abandoned paper cross his path, maybe tumbleweed.

His e-mail account is jammed with messages from the Home Office. Great work! Highest productivity of all the national offices! Interview requests from *Fortune*, *The Wall Street Journal*! Marketing has coined a phrase: the Johnson Pig Incentive. It's the latest business fad, the new barometer of 'making it,' but no other business can make the system work as effectively. They offer him a new position—Teleportational Specialist. Seminars, mini-courses, a series of instructional video tapes, an infomercial. A sketch of the book cover is faxed over: Johnson and a smiling pig, a strange, Oriental-esque land their background, a pup tent hanging lazily over Johnson's left shoulder. *Scientific American* wants a story.

Corkle's breath is warm and meaty from supper with his mother in Wyoming. Mother Corkle sent a note back with her son, attached to a homemade peach pie:

Dear Mr. Johnson,

My thanks for discovering a way my son can come spend some quality time with his dear old dam (though I'm sure he'll come to regret it when he realizes that he no longer has an excuse to miss family gatherings). Though I must admit, the whole thing confuses me—I always considered rabbits more a traveling animal (ha ha).

Again, my warmest thanks. I made Elvin promise to bring you by some time. I'm noted for my biscuits. Should be a good break from city food.

You should also meet Elvin's sister, Loretta. Elvin's told us a lot about you, and she'd love to meet you in person. She was engaged to the church organist, but it turns out he's going with the McAllott girl, Reemy. A hussy, if you ask me, who'll dump him for anyone with a better income.

Loretta's not like that at all, mind you. She's been brought up with all the commandments and a proper fear of God. Sounds to me you could stand meeting a proper woman.

God Bless,
Mother Corkle

P.S. May I call you Vince?

Johnson on the verge of tears. When was the last time someone called him Vince? He had no idea Corkle even knew his first name. Johnson is spent, eternal hangover, tired of finding desk drawers to piss in. He lets Corkle lead him to his own office, his secretary's OUT TO LUNCH developing cobwebs.

There sits a tent, maps (country, city, street) spread over the floor like drop cloths before a painting job. A squealing kennel shuddering by the oak desk.

"The first step," Corkle explains, "is to find a place. Picking a country is fine, but then you leave your landing completely to chance. That put Price in the middle of a pond—instant

13

pneumonia. The more you look over the maps, the better chance of hitting the spot you're looking for. Just thinking 'Washington D.C.' could land you in the Southeast, bad neighborhood, especially for well dressed whites." Corkle snorts once or twice and leads Johnson around the maps, making recommendations: a good Thai restaurant there, a good massage parlor, where to find a damn fine martini.

"You might want to start short," Corkle suggests, picking up a map of Florida, but Johnson feels he is encased in Plexiglas—shielded, covered with a crisp, transparent border he can't quite hear the world through, yet it keeps banging in at him, the thumps bothersome and painful. The only way to quiet it all is to follow along, and it is this Johnson does, numbly.

Corkle shows Johnson a map of northern Florida, a park outside Gainesville that is quiet and out of the way.

"Not even many gators," Corkle jokes, muffled to Johnson's ears.

A quick orientation on the best way to hold a pig (both arms wrapped lengthwise, one hand holding the forelocks, the other patting the hind). It wriggles, belts out a squeal that makes even Corkle cringe noticeably.

"It'll stop," Corkle assures. "Too small to fight too long."

Soon enough, the pig settles, and Johnson is helped down Indian-style, the pig snuggling affectionately against his chest. (Such a warm and friendly presence!) He scootches into the tent, all the while Corkle coaching:

"Just picture the place as concretely as you can, but don't make it up. Think of the map, what you saw on it. When you start going places, just remember where you been, and you can get back in an instant. Rumor has it Peterson in Research tried picturing a Bugs Bunny cartoon. Couldn't keep it too clear in his head, but for an instant, he said, he saw Technicolor out the tent flaps. No one's heard from him lately so I'd say don't try anything too risky."

As Corkle zips him in, Johnson has an instantaneous flash —a place in absence of everything. No noise. No needs. No deadlines, no supervision. The body no longer a body. A wonderful removal from everything. Johnson can only picture it as a freedom from his self, from everything he knows. He can't capture the idea and concentrate on it. It came upon him uncalled for, and left without restraint, but Johnson hopes it was with him just long enough.

"The transport is instantaneous. One second, you'll be hearing my voice, next you'll be there. Remember, it's the same thing to get back, just

The Book of Roger

Of course, just when you thought its storyline would fizzle into contentment, the Book of Roger—that third person limited omniscient narrative—is suffering an unexpected twist, isn't it, Roger? A tale of truckdriving, three-hundred-days-a-year-on-the-road Roger and his darling, quiet Rhonda, who dealt with loss and turbulent times in their early days when their first child gave up the ghost while still in his mother's womb. A decade later, Rhonda managed a successful birth, Herman, and at last there was a little one to fill the vacant crib you refused to get rid of and jiggle the rattle from its packaging. Five years later, another son, Darrell. Rhonda kept house in Quakertown and worked short hours at Walgreen's when Herman and Darrell were at school. You, Roger, sent cards and gifts on birthdays and important holidays. Herman went straight into the Air Force after graduation (Mountain Home, ID) and hasn't visited once. When Darrell was a senior in high school, Roger retired and used Rhonda's savings to close on a little house plopped into the center of an apple orchard in Beckett, NJ. With Darrell now a frosh at Rutgers, wasn't the Book of Roger supposed to fade off into an unexciting resolution?: Roger raising apples, Rhonda churning out apple butter, apple turnovers, baked apples with cinnamon, poached apple in a reduced port sauce, apple stuffing, etc. The two of them peaceful in their retirement, like Adam and Eve in their golden years, as they admired the sunset from adjacent rockers.

The tent caterpillar infestation seemed only a hindrance at first. Sure, Roger fought a losing battle: the hordes of sex lure traps overflowed in seconds, as did the Vaseline-smeared girdles wrapped around the trunks. He emptied out at least a dozen tanks of Super BT as the vermin wriggled through one slow, bile-filled death at a time. But the light rain of larvae droppings remained persistent and unabated.

No rocker-time could be had in that kind of rain. So Roger called the local distributor for a Sevin drop. He gave them his credit card number and scheduled the duster for just after dawn on the 24th. The distributor sent pamphlets full of thanks and instructions—evacuation of the premises for 48 hours, including household pets. The day before those blessed chemicals would come and wipe the orchard free of vermin, Roger taped the windows shut and made reservations for two at the Highlander Inn. A quick chemical wash, and the Book of Roger would be free to meet its anticlimactic end.

And then Rhonda's bomb, revising the Book of Roger from the beginning.

She announced over dinner the night before the Sevin drop that she was leaving for her sister's in Ohio and not coming back. Rhonda explained in a four-hour monologue that from her point of view their marriage ended when the first child was lost. Herman and Darrell helped soften the blow, but only a little. She had acquiesced to the relocation to another state and the loss of her savings to keep Darrell from further hardship after moving away from his school and friends.

This orchard never inspired an ounce of hope in her, Roger. Nor did she look at it as any kind of Eden. The gala apples came out sour and undersized. No one took them from the stand at the end of the driveway, even when left out for free. While she talked and explained and teared up, Roger stewed in confusion and silence. But she spoke at length in hopes that her husband would offer some explanations of his own and give her some insight into this man that she has seen as little more than a self-sustaining package. She never deluded herself into thinking that her dear Roger was absent of emotion, but she spoke at length to give him one last chance to reveal those emotions to her, to provide some kind of emotional "Hello, it's me" and expose what he'd hidden from her since she first knew him.

But that effort was a dismal failure, for all you did was stare at the table when she gave you openings to interrupt her. She has nothing left to offer now on the night she is leaving except an occasional "Excuse me" when her (now) ex-husband happens to be in her path while she and Darrell haul boxes out to her Volvo—yes, Roger, the boy came down from college to help his mother leave you. You could offer something more of a response than a dumb gesture of letting her go first when you get in her way.

Here is the full truth, Roger—Rhonda is tired of being the sole member of this marriage still grieving over what was, in the Book of Roger, nothing more than an unfortunate circumstance ages ago. In the Book of Roger, the first child wasn't worth all of Rhonda's tears because it was never even born and so could not have died. Roger never bothered noticing how much Rhonda had reconstructed her life around the expectation of a child only to lose him ('lose' was the doctor's terminology, as though a child could be a set of keys). You never thought the first child ever existed, but Rhonda named him. And she named him after his father, so imagine how she felt when Roger, Jr. was buried and Roger, Sr. never visited the site. Roger, Sr. never acknowledged his suffix and instead went back on the road and thought that doing so was providing for his wife, since there were hospital bills and funeral expenses to make good on. And you insisted that she not get rid of the crib and the unopened toys should your luck improve next time. Rhonda had to deal with her grief and abandonment and vacuous home all on her own. Face it, Roger—Roger, Sr. has been too much a wanderer in his own life. Might as well call him Ishmael—a naive man looking for a ship to sail, ignorant to the dangers of the crew around him, as well as the uselessness of his mission.

Put the evidence together, Roger: Rhonda's detachment, both in conversation and bed, for a decade before she would agree to get pregnant again; her tears when she looked at little, squirming Herman; her insistence that the child sleep in bed with mom and dad, even when dad was fresh off the road and hadn't been with his wife in months. The children became perfect excuses to avoid all relations with her husband. Wasn't it obvious that she was more animated with Herman and Darrell than with the man she married? She has been more at ease with that gravestone than at home—of course she has visited it, Roger. Even when Roger, Sr. blew Rhonda's savings on some sudden wish to be an apple-farmer, Rhonda crossed the river and up 276 to visit that grave instead of those day trips to Atlantic City she lied about. She confided her unshared unhappiness to that chiseled slab of marble, and soon she found another confidant in the third fruit of her womb: blonde and bright-faced Darrell.

While Roger, Sr. labored in the orchard, Rhonda told her youngest about his lost older brother and the emptiness of her marriage. When Darrell left for college, he knew the future better than his own dad, and he knew on whose side he was going to stand. Now back to help his mother move out her things, he takes pleasure in his father's broken-back stance and loss for words whenever he finds himself in Rhonda's path. Herman is as much a lost cause as Roger, Jr. for support—he requested assignment in Idaho because he wanted a good excuse to never come home again. Roger, Sr. created kin who are as distant from him as galaxies, red-shifting away from him as fast as the laws of momentum will allow.

So this is how the book ends, Roger: Rhonda leaves with Darrell and a trunkload of her things (all that she would ever want to remind her of married life), and when the night starts easing up in the east, Roger, Sr. finds himself alone, all alone. He tears open all the windows he had taken such time to seal and mans his rocker on the front porch, the front door wide open. He is not going to leave. This house, this orchard, was to be his gift to his wife and children. Even if none of them want another thing to do with him for the rest of their lives, he is going to cleanse it of this plague. When he sees the duster approach, he notes its glare when it reflects the morning beams. The single-prop craft shines with as much brilliance as the DDT truck did, the one that used to drive through little Roger, Sr.'s neighborhood, its rear apparatus atomizing that precious chemical that was at the time the savior of mankind, able to kill all the malicious insects and germs in the whole world. Little Roger, Sr. and his friends ran behind the truck and breathed in lungfuls of the stuff. It was the cleanest smell in the world, wasn't it, Roger? And when the duster lets loose its goods, the cloud of Sevin hangs in the air like an amorphous paratrooper.

Imagine being in the midst of that cloud, Roger. Imagine wafting down to obliterate the infestation in those trees. That cloud is the shape of a last stab at hope, Roger, and it is as lethal as hope has proven. Wish for no sudden change of wind speed or current. Let the cloud go where it has to. Continue this course. Accept this dreadful end.

Together, the Choir Grows Old

We cling to our musical history. A thousand motets, responsoria and cantata we have performed in our combined career. Still, we move ever forward. Canon and improvisation we sing alike. A lifetime of training in our every breath.

We have a toy poodle we walk when we are barren of inspiration. We listen intently to the astonishment of passersby elicited by our poodle dyed the hue of a bruised pistachio, our poodle named Giuseppe in honor of all Italians in the world.

"Aww," these passersby cry, and we await the perfect intonation to inspire us to our grand opus, 32 Variations on the Theme of Aww. We arrange ourselves like the pipes of an organ—our minds tuned perfectly, our throats hoarse from too many cigarettes and the occasional mound of chew. We are making music as we speak: notes and bars and refrains and movements. We are vocalizing our passions in high C's and the rest of our limited alphabet. We sing of bricks and refrigerators and Cadillacs overcome with rust.

Back home, we indulge in danish and petite-four and sticky bun, all washed down with hot chocolate made from powder (three packets per 8 oz. cup for the sweetest, absolutely sweetest mixture), for as our bodies get denser and denser and bend the floorboards with our ever-increasing weight we feel our communal voice rise to even vaster heavens. We chime together in a most solid note, a most unwavering note, a note that drives others to drink for want of such beauty. We conspire to melodious greatness. We understand their envy and we weep and wail for them in wondrous vocal clarity; we mourn for their unachievable goals, our Stabat Mater accompanied by yellow crumbs erupting from between our teeth.

Day's end, we wear cloned flannel nightgowns and we travel upstairs in an elliptical cluster, our steps in perfect rhythm so not one of us knees another in the backside. Candles held reverently before us, we sing of nightingales and crickets and the way fog settles in ghostly manner when darkness falls.

"Nightingales and crickets," we sing, "and the way fog settles in ghostly manner when darkness falls."

"Ghostly manner," the baroque section of us echoes.

This is our opera, our day inhaled and exhaled in exquisite musicality. We huff out our collective lights and we settle to sleep, to rest. We drift off with a hum, the like of which skylarks dream.

The Cat Strangler

The usual growls erupt when the Cat Strangler removes tonight's feline from its kennel by the scruff. Tabbies, Manx, Siamese, Russian Blues: all have been the Cat Strangler's plaything at one time or another.

A slight struggle, a couple practice squeezes and others methods of impersonal handling, and off he goes. The neighborhood shrugs its collective set of shoulders in hope of shutting out the yowls and the hisses stretched into high pitch by the Cat Strangler's strong, trained hands (rumor has it he worked in a Kosher slaughterhouse once, cutting sheep suspended by their ankles, putting the saw to cows). Parents turn up their televisions; children pull on the pillows over their heads to the point of near suffocation. Household pets break into instinctual runs, scratch at doors or windows that impede their progress or flee into unfamiliar territory, their name tags with phone number their only hope of return now.

The Cat Strangler continues his performance. It can last an hour, sometimes only a few minutes. These time frames are not the cat's choice. The neighbors call authorities, and the authorities stammer helplessly—they've been over all this before (the pulling up, the getting out, the knocking on the door, only to be met with the Cat Strangler's cat-strangling credentials, signed by officious names under University patronage).

For what few seem to hear under the barrage of kitty torture is the Cat Strangler's wife, Jill, in accompaniment (tonight's episode: Heinrich Ignaz Franz Von Biber (1644-1705), Sonata for Violin and Basso Continuo in C minor). No one bothers appreciating how a firm grip on the neck and a harsh pull of the tail makes a perfect B flat, how a good, tight squeeze produces a high E.

Instead, psychiatrists will be consulted—nightmares will be related, trauma will be diagnosed, tears will be shed. Parents will explain to their children the wrongdoings of the Cat Strangler's art form; they will recite scripture; they will make moral imperatives. Animal activists, lurking in the shadows, will lick bloodlust from their lips and draw up plans of attack; red paint on fat, fur-clad wives will be nothing compared to this. Far off in distant, political lands, untouched by the screams of dying cats but active just the same, government agencies will do the voodoo they do, their deliberation fueled by recordings of the Cat Strangler's feline realizations of the classics, piped through the Congressional sound system like feedback. Nothing will remain the same.

But for now, the recital ends—to no applause.

Jill critiques her husband's performance. Siamese, she believes, have too harsh an overall tone for something as technically precise as Biber. For Shostakovich or Schnittke, fine (or even Tchaikovsky or most any of the other Russians), but for the Germans she is more inclined towards the long hairs. Jill removes her performance gown as she expresses her thoughts; she puts away her cello while wearing only undergarments—her husband gets so caught up in his work, he needs distraction.

The Cat Strangler makes hurried notes for his treatise while Jill entices him to the bedroom—such a landmark work it will be! His professors had little hope for Musica Zoocidia beyond music school experimentation, and certainly with animals no wilder than your typical, bred-into-submission laboratory rat. The Cat Strangler's treatise will break all confines! He sees a future in pig concertos—nay, even a day where the Echo Sonata for Himalayan, Chihuahua and ostrich is a practical feasibility.

He deposits the spent instrument in a brown paper bag in unceremonious fashion. He drives it to a deep wood, as far as his car will allow, and empties the bag onto a pile of expired feline brethren, cats piled upon cats piled upon cats piled upon cats, tongues stuck out in strangulation horror. As the ones in the least of the heap become possessed with maggots, the whole pile writhes in minute rhythm: swaying, even...though maybe not. The minions of certain manufacturers of sporting equipment raid this pile of former felines, and they ship them to foreign sweatshops for the making of tennis rackets of the old-fashioned kind, the kind from before the chemical and plastic revolutions. These rackets are placed into the able hands of gleaming white tennis players, who swing into furious volleys for game.

The Fine Art of Fletcherism

This morning, the golden anniversary of his flight from Germany, Doctor Josef Mengele is trying to sort himself out inside a palm-leaf hut among rain forest natives in the Amazon. Dawn is near. Mengele lies awake next to a native woman who wears two white stones around her neck. The stones look like bulbs of dried clay, but they are stones, and they are almost identical in size, but up close it can be seen that the left one is slightly larger. Mengele does not know this woman's name, or the tribe's name, or their language (he has only been with them five months), and he does not know how these primitive people managed to bore holes in these smooth and round and almost bleach-white stones. The stones clacked together loudly when this woman was on top of Mengele, but now they are quiet, the woman sleeping and dreaming of flight, of trees and vines melding into an exhilarating blur of greens and oranges as she rushes past them, while Mengele trembles beside her, feeling lonesome and hated among these natives who are his salvation only because they do not know who he is.

Mengele was at one time overwhelmed by how the women of this tribe offered themselves to him, this unnaturally pale man who emerged like a god from the burning wreck of two ships, Nazi hunters in one, Mengele's trusted henchmen in the other. The husbands in this tribe are honored if Mengele takes their wives, and they are keeping score, the current leader honored with a necklace of white stones. Fathers try to tempt him with descriptions of their daughters. There is a great emphasis on the ears, their size and length of lobe. They want to give Mengele their virgins, because men in this tribe don't want girls who were not desired by other men. Pregnant women are much sought-after as brides, especially if the child is Mengele's. The women in this tribe wear palm-leaf earmuffs and nothing else, the leaves covering their most erotic places, and they willingly undress their heads for him.

All Mengele has left from his years of hiding is a white silk robe from a Brazilian resort, an F on the lapel, that hangs, a ghost on the wall, across the hut. A breeze Mengele cannot feel makes the robe stir. The sleeves rock slightly, almost as if sashaying, and Mengele stands abruptly, quickly, despite his old bones and atrophied muscles, and he gathers the robe in his arms and leaves the hut. He needs no more ghosts. Mengele misses the comfort of ignorance, when concerns of money shortages or improperly prepared blowfish were more daunting than the threat of capture. Though he knew there were experienced hunters after him, hunters who had their pictures in international newspapers for catching comrades like Hess and Barbie and Eichmann, they were but two-dimensional figures to Mengele then, images that did not breathe or aim rifles or wear mustaches. Mengele once lay by poolsides, Auschwitz but a fading memory, the twins nearly forgotten, and servants and maids and bellhops called him 'Sir.' Outside, in the penultimate dark that reduces the village to a circle of hut-shaped shadows with crimson freckles at the hub in the dying fire, Mengele hurls the robe into the river. He watches it float onto the water, then jerk and bandy as it is pecked at and worried by vigilant piranha. Mengele urinates into the river, careful not to step on the catfish stuffed with insects and berries that he knows the husband of the woman with the white stones has left by the opening of his hut. His flesh, still pallid despite months of walking naked in the sun, seems to glow in the dark, and Mengele feels like a beacon, or a target flare.

He looks up at the ceiling of trees above him and remembers in *National Geographic* how millions of new species of insects were found in that canopy of branches that spreads for thousands of miles all around him. Sometimes, Mengele swears he can feel the ground moving, teeming with life, and when this happens, he wants to kneel, put his hands to the ground and whisper into the black, damp, rich soil to coax all burrowing life beneath him to rise. He wants the worms to run between his toes, the roots to wrap themselves around his ankles. He wants them all to forgive him, for he swears never to kill again. Insects land on his flesh and bite him, but Mengele is making himself accustomed to this by not swatting them, despite the itch.

The river creeps soundlessly, without waves or even minor laps up against the banks, but still the remnants of the two ships Mengele can barely see in the dark are slowly being washed away. He finishes pissing and feels relieved, though not completely at ease. False leads planted here and there, a bogus death, a fake tombstone purposefully inscribed with an alias all too easy to figure out and a body alike in stature and even dental work were all not enough to assuage the hunters or the man with the black mustache and pith helmet who had Mengele in his rifle sight when both ships erupted into fire. The explosion sent Mengele into the air, straight up almost. He felt the heat as the clothes on his body burned, and he landed in a soft pile of fallen palm leaves. Insects and birds scattered from the pile. Mengele heard the captain's mate—a three-fingered Brazilian teenager who could shoot bananas one-by-one from a bunch—jump from the burning hull of Mengele's ship and swim only a couple of strokes before being eaten by the piranha.

The sound of the boy screaming was ghastly at first—inhuman, high-pitched, all too reminiscent of many, many deaths—but the screaming quickly stopped, and Mengele heard the boy moan, as if the pain had become something sexual, the piranha bites more like kisses. Mengele is surprised that he admires these men, even the man with the black mustache: their lives ended in a simple stroke.

Piranha do not attack these natives. They can swim among the small fish with ghastly teeth, but Mengele knows the piranha would strip him in seconds, he is so small and scrawny now, so insignificant. There has been talk among the men in the village of making Mengele chief, but they have decided not to tell him this yet. Seven women are already starting to show, and the men predict there will be babies with fair skin. They want to make Mengele more than chief—they want to make him father. They want to put a crown of palm bark around his penis.

The sound of an airplane far overhead is not uncommon here anymore, civilization a week's walk away, but the sound still scares Mengele, and when he hears a plane this morning, he becomes erect instantly. He runs inside his hut and mounts and enters the woman with the white stones before she can fully wake. He thrusts so hard he starts to cry, and he tells her, "I'm found, I'm found," and the woman laughs (Mengele's penis is small), laughs at this surprise, this gift at such an appropriate time. Mengele rolls over, pulling the woman on top of him, and the stones clack against each other metronomically. This woman is one of Mengele's last pleasures, he is sure of it. There is no leaving this place. The hunters killed in the fire have friends who work in offices and can find out what hotel Mengele had to escape from late at night and what boat he smuggled himself onto. Even at his peak, near orgasm, the stones knocking furiously now, Mengele expects to be shot. He expects men to run into his hut and unleash on him fifty years of anger and hatred. Even when he doesn't die and is finished, Mengele passes out from the strain, though the woman with the white stones is fully awake now and ready for more.

Mengele dreams quickly nowadays, almost as soon as his eyes close, but this time is worse than usual, dream after dream, nightmares in succession. He dreams of the twins at Auschwitz, their long black hair magnificent again, and those gorgeous Jewish noses! Mengele can watch both these twins at the same time in his dream, each cell half his vision. The experiment is working perfectly, as it does only in his dreams. He makes love to one twin, the other looks at him lovingly; he feeds one steak, the other a bowl of sewage, and the one with the steak refuses to eat. Mengele wakes with this brown woman beside him, and he feels unclean, the memory of those young, white, underexposed and undernourished Jewish bodies still vivid.

There are signs of other white men. The chief of the tribe has a leather motorcycle jacket, almost indiscernible under the leaf covering he puts over it so he can wear it in the rain, and behind one of the huts is a pile of empty Lady Lee orange drink half-pint containers, left out to attract bugs that the natives pick at for the orange flavor that sticks to them. Mengele is sure he has seen marks in the jungle where camera tripods once stood, and grooves on the riverbank where boats may have landed. Sometimes natives from another village come running into the center of the huts. They fart and run back. The natives here get angry and hold their breaths, the smell infectious, they think, if allowed to enter their bodies. They send warriors out to retaliate. Mengele sometimes thinks of going out himself, to find a real town where he can turn himself in, but he knows the terrain would quickly get all too unfamiliar, and he would never find his way back.

Mengele tries again to enter the woman pressed against him, and he tries to imagine her as one of his twins, but her smell is all wrong: this woman is experienced and loose. The sun is now up fully and he can see her too well. Mengele has been inside this woman several times before, and she knows how to take him. *I need this*, Mengele tells himself. *I need this*. He chose this woman by staring at her. He entered the circle around the village fire and spoke German to the natives because they do not care about his nationality. *"Eine schreckliche Nacht!"* He could barely remember his own language, he had kept it hidden so long. The natives smiled at him. *"Nicht Dawk, es ist ja meine Pflicht!"* To a man laughing:

"Aha! Das geht mich an." The women waited anxiously for Mengele to choose, and as he looked them over, as though he were shopping for apples, he sang:

> *Der Vogelfänger bin ich ja,*
> *Stets lustig, heisa, hopsassa!*
> *Ich Vogelfänger bin bekannt*
> *Bei alt und jung in ganzen Land.*
> *Weiß mit dem Locken umzugehn*
> *Und mich auf's Pfeifen zu verstehn.*
> *Drum kann ich froh und lustig sein,*
> *Denn alle Vögel sind ja mein.*

Though the woman with the white stones was older, her body starting to sag, Mengele stared at the white stones shining in the firelight long enough that the woman's husband cried out in victory, and he took Mengele by the hand and led him back to his hut while his wife pulled on her ears, preparing herself.

Mengele hopes that the women he has impregnated will give birth mostly to boys, Aryan and Brazilian both, and two girls would make a nice ratio. Mengele wonders how many of the children are going to have his nose, his straight forehead, though none will carry his name. There are no twins in this tribe. Mengele is not sure if it is something in the genes, or if twins are taboo here, a bad omen, taken immediately to the river and fed to the piranha while they are still too young to be protected by the jungle. He can picture the headlines—TRIBE OF JOSEF MENGELE LOOK-ALIKES FOUND IN DEEPEST RAIN FOREST! He wonders if this is the legacy he can leave behind, and not the one of the Nazi butcher, waving impoverished souls right or *links*, his greatest concern the rhythm at which he swung his decision-making baton back and forth, his sentences for the haggard, obedient Jews determined mostly by tempo.

But there is the white man who came into the village five nights ago, three hours after everyone awoke to the sound of a failing engine and a crash barely a mile away. The entire village but Mengele stared as this man, almost thirty, blond, blue-eyed, Swedish descent possibly, bleeding from the ears and littered with bug bites, passed out upon reaching the first hut. He wore a pilot's jacket and boots, and he had a pistol on his hip, .38 caliber, enough to make Mengele shiver.

Of course, Mengele killed him. The women surrounded this new man, admired him, even the women who were carrying Mengele's children, and they took him into an empty hut and cleaned him up. They laid him on a straw mat, much as they had done when Mengele first came to the village, and they left water and a stuffed fish for the Swede if he ever woke up. In the dark, the village fire out and everyone else asleep, Mengele went in with a rock and pounded the Swede's head until there was nothing left to pound. Then he dragged the mat and body to the river, his own head turned away in disgust, and dropped them in.

The taking of the rock to the young man is still fresh in Mengele's memory, and how the blood looked black in the moonlight. Somehow, Mengele gets himself back to sleep, though dreaming is no relief at all.

The twins are both pregnant, and Mengele cuts them open to see if they are each giving birth to twins. This is not fair, he hears himself scream. This is memory, not dream, and he wakes up, he thinks, sweating, the dead pilot's blood everywhere, too fresh a kill, a single fetus in each hand. The mothers, lacking the benefits of anesthetic, writhe and scream in unison, *Why?*

Mengele wakes again, his head on the native woman's chest, and the metaphor of the white stones is far too obvious—they are of different sizes and shapes, but there is no denying that they are white stones, cut from the same rock, despite how different they may appear to be. Mengele has to break through a wall to escape, since he can't remember the way out anymore. The hut collapses, and the woman with the white stones screams, muffled under straw. She screams her word for father, and the rest of the village wakes and screams in response, dark forms exiting their huts, but father has already jumped into the river.

The fish do not attack at first. In the morning light, Mengele sees them encompass him and watch him with

35

fright, or maybe disgust, though Mengele would like to think they are afraid of him. The whole village is at the riverbank, their hands extended in praise and welcome, welcoming father into their numbers at last, but Mengele won't accept this. He taunts the piranha, splashing the water, offering his left leg, a shank, a thin, paltry arm, but they don't advance just yet.

"*Roust!*" Mengele screams. He fears the natives will begin jumping in the water after him. He fears they will carry him back to the village, build him a new hut, feed him all the stuffed fish he can eat, and that he will never be able to get away from them.

"*Wir haben keine Minute zu versäumen,*" screams Mengele, and at this the piranha attack. The pain is too quick for Mengele, too severe. He is being pulled apart into bite-sized chunks, and it is excruciating. He remembers the captain's mate, and he wonders when the pleasure will begin. "*'s ist umsonst! Es ist vergebens!*" Half of his body has been eaten away in a matter of seconds. Mengele feels pain everywhere, even in the bits of flesh already taken away. His flesh is swimming away from him, being actively fletcherized, spreading out into the water beyond his reach, hiding under roots, being digested and shat, extending into the rain forest, becoming a part of everything, and the pain is too much. Mengele screams, he screams, he wants his body back together.

Soup

The soup man was ready to gnaw his way out of his own skin. The three homeless women—who lived under the soup man's back porch and were paid the occasional dollar to sample his creations—knew not what to do about it themselves.

The walls of the soup man's kitchen had transformed into the sides of humongous chickens, feathers black and red and falling at a regular pace, as if four enlarged poultry had been sewn together by an even larger chicken master. The corners of the room came together in seamless corners of pocked and pliable flesh. The breast meat framing the door bulged as if hanging over a belt cinched too tightly. The soup man had to fight and scrape to open his very own door, and the homeless women sucked on the hair growing beneath their bottom lips as they peered through the window and wondered at the significance of this portent.

The soup man wept with bitterness and frustration, for not only had the feathers dropped into a thick, downy allergic nightmare, but all the soup man's soups were tainted with the taste of this overrated bird, even the turtle garlic gumbo, the Zimbabwe peanut butter garnished with broiled tofu, the tomato leek with cucumber and matzo balls served with a side of Dionysus grape Jell-O.

Customers bellowed their dissatisfaction. They seethed over the pots of cabbage and onion with diced pork that tasted distinctly of chicken. Restaurants vacated due to the sudden banality of the *du jour*. The homeless soup tasters pecked away at each other inquisitively—"Why is this? Why is this?" Those who were once connoisseurs of the soup man's creations wandered aimlessly, their palates vapid. They muttered to themselves, "It tastes like chicken. Chicken. It tastes like chicken." A tumor sprouted on the soup man's neck, straight and true and rectangular, as though a miniature Winnebago were erupting from his sinews, and the soup man stopped answering the complaints about another batch of chicken soup. A deluge of electronic rings, their screams no longer heeded. The soup man named his kitchen walls Myron, Coventry, Adlai and Papageno, and he spent his days telling them of what marvelous soups he once made: cold peach served in a taco bowl with vanilla ice cream; okra and green pepper with three barbecued gizzards floating on top; halibut and hamburger in a thick, creamy celery broth. The three homeless women fell into sibylline paroxysms of hunger, while Myron the chicken wall shivered restlessly under the soup man's gentle caresses...

Self-Interview

Q: So what's wrong with you, anyway?

A: This is absurd! I did not come here to be raked across coals for your amusement! If you wish proper discourse in a civilized Q&A format, I am willing to abide, but such attacks—

Q: Okay, okay...

A: —will hardly be tolerated. That you can lay money on.

Q: Understood. Truce?

A: Truce.

Q: Again?

A: If you wish.

Q: And so...

A: Proper, this time, I remind you.

Q: Most proper. Seat?

A: Thanks so very much.

Q: No problem. Anything else?

A: I assure you, I am quite comfortable.

Q: To begin?

A: Again?

Q: By all means.

A: Then by all means. By all means, then.

Q: Then, your childhood.

A: ...ah-ah ah ah...

Q: No, no, not an attack at all.

A: You do plan to edit this before publication, don't you?

Q: Why open myself up to criticism for a slovenly effort?

A: I didn't think you could stand the reputation.

Q: It would be a bear. To be thought of as loose...

A: ...out of control...

Q: ...unconscious.

A: Random, even.

Q: Don't make me cringe. Shall we begin?

A: Certainly, every writer seeks a seamless narrative. In other words, one seeming to arise from nature rather than contrivance. Oddly enough, every writer seeks credit for being able to contrive the seemingly noncontrived.

Q: Most certainly.

A: For certainly a writer such as you, who slaves at his craft to offer a completely tamed text whose trickery, dancing and card tricks should seem more spontaneous than sculpted, seeks at least a modicum of credit for your efforts to produce such a façade of a lack of effort. But if your effort is to be absent from the creation, so to speak, how are you to reap your reward?

Q: The endless trap.

A: The ends seem unattainable, don't they?

Q: Eternally receding, to be sure.

A: Worth the effort?

Q: Not if you justify the effort only by the attainment of awards...

A: And rewards.

Q: ...and rewards.

A: But what else would such an effort be made for?

Q: The effort should be made, ideally, for the sake of the effort.

A: Cut that down a clause and you have yourself a bumper sticker. Surely you don't find yourself believing that?

Q: In my best moments, I do.

A: What are the best moments?

Q: The moments when I am in the midst of the effort, of course.

A: And the worst?

Q: The moment after the effort is complete.

A: Then what?

Q: Then it's all sell, sell, *sell*.

A: I sympathize.

Q: I'm doubtful. You recently wrote a story where twelve gnomes must tote a giant banana through endless tundra for a hundred years as punishment for excessive nose-picking. Where in all of that are we to identify an effort towards noncontrived narrative?

A: How do you know of such a thing?

Q: Do you deny that you recently completed such a story?

A: 'Complete' is such a final term.

Q: Even if not completed: where in this conceit is the opportunity for the reader to empathize with something familiar?

A: There is something familiar there for all, I'd imagine.

Q: An eighty-foot banana? Twelve gnomes with raw nostrils dragging it along?

A: Beloved, you make it all so cut and dry. It's more complicated than this, you know. The issue is as complicated as seamless, natural life is complicated: one of those poor fellows deviated his own septum with his incessant fingering.

Q: Where begins the seamless, natural course of events in all that? It all seems as everyday as genetically enhanced snails competing in a polo tournament.

A: I like that idea...

Q: You will credit me, of course?

A: Wouldn't have it any other way...but back to the matter at hand. The seam is beneath the opening of the wound, of course. When one's world is startled from orbit, one tends not to appreciate the new orbital path but seeks avidly for details that remind him of the old one. When we are cast into the unfamiliar, we pay little mind to the unfamiliar details and cling like mad to whatever is familiar. Therein lies a great advantage for hiding a seam and make the world seem seamless. I described aptly the nostril pain our self-deviated dwarf experienced. Almost any reader has felt the pain of one pick too many, and so I hogtie him to my world with that empathy.

Q: But wherefore a banana? Surely a spiky pear or even an elephantine turkey drumstick would serve such a purpose just as nicely. Where's the necessity that says a banana must be here and no other fruit?

A: The universe *is* a confine, beloved. The banana serves to open the wound only in that it is a ball and chain to the droning gnomes. But despite being huge and a method of contrition, it is a banana after all. That much is certain, and that much lets all who wish to know that there is still a familiar world here after all, for we know what a banana is just as much as we can empathize with having picked our own noses too much.

Q: But what of the spiky pear?

A: How real is a spiky pear to you? Have you looked on it in choice produce aisles as a sincere possibility for refreshment or as a wax-like oddity?

Q: Well, if you're going to put it that way...

A: And a drumstick?! Can you even start to consider the intricacies of dragging carved poultry? Must the dwarves retrieve straggling strips as part of their penance? And from which end should they drag it? From the end of the bone, or do they fashion some kind of harness around the severed joint? And would the skin still cling through the endless dragging? Tell me, if you were sentenced to move a hormonal banana, where would seem the most natural place to start pulling it from?

Q: The stem, of course, provided it has been broken from its bunch with proper care.

A: There. You see? An image alienating and homey both.

Q: But gnomes?

A: Would you prefer miniature rhinosceri with little sense of etiquette? But then, how do they go about picking at their nostrils? Some kind of land-bound squid, then. Those tentacles must provide endless temptation to stick them into any available orifice. How about miniaturized Richard

Nixon clones? But wouldn't these demand even the slightest scientific rationale? Can we afford to take so long to familiarize the audience with the unfamiliar?

Q: Point well taken. I suppose you'll say a story should be clear of its intents within the first five syllables.

A: Pshaw. I wouldn't even give it that long. If the title doesn't set the world into its spin in a precise trajectory, the effort is clearly in trouble from the get-go...

Mercy

I alight.

I rest my baseball cap on the seat cushion for the time of the alighting, though not before a brisk shake to avoid as much as humanly possible a rim-wide ring of wet where I am to eventually deposit myself into sitting position and face her once again. Here she is, she is here waiting, waiting she is, and to make her wait further for the natural removal of unwanted wet before I can sit is testing her most benevolent patience. The rain has done its duty, done its damage, done its due, and I take this opportunity of enclosure to offer myself a respite from the precipitation and take the offer offered for some drying out.

Position of cap: brim forward, team mascot (team of no consequence) still smiling after all these years.

Thus having laid, I remove my first layer—rayon windbreaker, black. It resists against my bulked sleeves, but no no no no no no *no* its sleeves will not reverse on me. An unfortunately uncomfortable position aids in the prevention of this reversal, a position reminiscent of rude detention in a legal manner, opposite hand holding the cuff of the sleeve being wriggled out of.

Patience patience, it comes, it comes off.

Source of legal simile: not from experience. Really. Please... let's be serious here.

Worthy note: windbreaker removal performed with concentrated care and not indicative of coming endeavors in the preparation of a prolonged sit. Reversed windbreaker sleeves, reversed black windbreaker sleeves especially, are for certain an ill omen and create chaos and turmoil and most certainly an abortion of the sitting procedure for sure for I would be a sitting duck for any doomsday meteor headed my way.

So permit the extended performance of windbreaker removal.

Windbreaker off, it must be folded and held and not placed on the back of the chair immediately. *Prevention of the following:* bottom of the heap. A loss of an opportunity for drying it out. This makes the process more intricate, more time-consuming, but to go back out there with a wet windbreaker and lose the opportunity for some drying out...

My order expressed to the waiting waiter: Coffee, I'll take coffee. Black coffee. Black coffee as strong a coffee as can be.

Windbreaker folded over (outside showing only, you bet), then folded over my arm, I remove flannel, tee, thermal, tee, long sleeve tee, tee, tee, always with care to prevent reversals, but always with more care not to drop the windbreaker—the dropping of a mere undergarment is an easy risk if the windbreaker is not to drop.

There are rules; always, there are rules.

Layers swathed, draped, drooped, hung. The windbreaker graces the top, some great black father out to smother his seed. Thus, chaos is curtailed, disaster on hold. I place the cap on a corner of the backrest and prepare for the sitting.

We will not go into detail here: this is just a sitting down, plain and simple—I will not concern much with the sitting. Sitting is natural, of nature, and may be done w/natural manner and mannerism.

Seated thus, clothes hung thus, donning still my final tee and wet wet trousers and lame excuses for shoes, coffee served thus (looking strong, kinda strong, could be stronger, all requests for milk, cream, sugar, a dash of cinnamon on top *confound these places!* refused flatly and the more I'm asked the more I have to turn the cup one full revolution for every no, every no spoken and every no screamed inside, a lot to make up for already), I am sitting and facing her, she angelic in her patience through my necessary goings-through, though who could meet a sister's eyes, a nun's eyes, meeting like this?

"Tell me how you are," she says, impossible to divine the intent. Sarcasm? Sincere concern? She is generally prone to the earnest, but still but still. Hard to know, hard like this, with the table so out of order and all, the salt and centerpiece and pepper in that order but far from a straight line based upon their centers of gravity (the only noncontestable point of reference for determining a straight line in table settings), and the sugar the sugar oh we haven't even started with the sugar, served in packets no less, such a confounded place this is, such a dump and a dive and a waste of her and my time, our time, mine and hers...

Yes, hard to gauge her request under such circumstances, quite hard, and I reply thus whilst drawing upon the table some hope of a sense of order amongst its decorations:

"Is this to curry favor?" I begin. "A cry for reconciliation, or a mere opener to maintain relationships ascertained and continued by our last conjoining also initiated previously by you by request sent through channels of my known habitation and habits of walking, stopping for a moment precisely for a look or a visage, a request effected along I'm certain with pecuniary remediation for there is little other reason for these channels to pass along your request and for what reason you would effect these communiqués is beyond me beyond me completely beyond me it is for what would you want a conjoinance? surely not only to ask that stupid stupid *stupid* question." Thus do I go too far when I open my mouth.

My hands shake and I continue the positioning positioning repositioning of aforementioned out-of-place items. Best I can I try to hold off the shaking but she must see it, but she knows enough of me to know to await an opening before speaking.

I continue.

"Unless we are to just resume where, they say," I quote, "'we left off,'" I unquote, "I quote, I unquote, in which case I am then to have a clear idea, then, of that time when, then, our conversation last ceased and thus pick it up from whence I left, or you left to be precise, yes, for you left and that is certain, you are the one who had enacted the leaving—"

My shuffling creates an imbalance in the sedentary nature of the salt shaker, and it falls and sprinkles white salt upon the white-like-salt tablecloth (confound *confound* confound), but there is no mistaking the presence of each and every granule there, mocking me there, announcing itself there with bells and whistles and the threat of mass destruction everywhere. It makes me want to scream.

And I am ready to.

She seizes the opportunity. "Norman," she says (she knows better than to take my hands). "Norman, we haven't forsaken you."

While I still taste salt I continue pressing pressing my fingers against the tablecloth, pressing them and licking them clean. Salt is bad, bad for the constitution, for the steadily-beating heart, yet all the salt must go, go away, and I continue while I still taste salt.

Meanwhile, she goes on again about the church, the love that is always there for me, the they who will love me and anoint me and clean me and take me into their fold evermore without death.

We'll care for you, Norman," she says. "We'll love you, Norman," she says. "You have only to ask us into your heart," she says, Norman.

Always they she speaks of, always the first person plural plural plural. Nothing personal, only collective.

"Marry me marry me marry me marry me marry me marry me marry me marry me marry me." I am permitted but one breath, a breath long enough only to skip one 'marry me' and keep my tempo is all that's permitted for any chance of success to remain. "Marry me marry me marry me marry me marry me marry me."

She puts out her hand and she is smiling, smiling in that conciliatory way, that way of no, that way of no, I'm sorry I'm sorry sorry saw-ree.

I don't take her hand and she ups to leave.

"Get yourself something to eat," she says. "Make sure you eat," and she leaves behind the usual amount. She leaves it on my side of the table.

I look at her. That angelic face. Literally.

She smiles. She bows her head, as if sliding down a ramp to propel her egress. She nods back to those who nod to her reverently.

She's doing her job.

I drink my coffee in the usual full-committal fashion. No stopping once the act is started. Burnage in the past has not been infrequent if the coffee does not cool at the expected rate.

This time, the drinking is the usual fire going down into me. The fire I can handle.

Payment made, her change pocketed (so much more pickled pork could be had for this amount versus the squandering that would ensue from maintaining the tab at this confounded place), rising and dressing and keeping windbreaker for final layer without exposure of same-material lining much the same as the process for the reverse, the actions by rote by rote by careful careful rote, I prepare to finish out the day.

My exit: damp only and clothed.

O the sun! Misty humidity and cold fronts pushing along heady heady clouds in return, in exposure, covet it no more. It is magnificent! It is blinding! I am blinded! Still, I maintain the motion I must make, my steps measured and necessary to transport me to where I may alight of this money as prodigiously as possible. Pig's knuckles pig's knuckles, pig's knuckles await. My eyes are burning! My lids are scorched. I trudge on, lest all come down around me.

Apples

If a man has lost a leg or an eye, he knows he has lost a leg or an eye; but if he has lost a self—himself—he cannot know it, because he is no longer there to know it.
—Oliver Sacks, *The Man Who Mistook His Wife for A Hat*

It was a falling dream, quick and sudden and scary. My alarm clock woke me, though I couldn't remember why I had set it. I forgot many things: people's names, the way back from the corner drugstore, the alphabet sometimes. I forgot how to pronounce words like 'photography' and 'knight,' but I didn't worry about it—the State paid for my house. It came with a houselady who cooked lunch and helped with the chores.

The night before I finished the Popov at Joey's and watched the Late Nite Movie, Channel 8, WMUT. Vampires, trapped underground for centuries by Renaissance vampire hunters, emerge in modern London and look for revenge. Being trapped was the part that scared me: locked in a cold box, no room to move for all those years. I drank by myself— Joey didn't want any, hadn't wanted any for a while now, and he went to bed early. It was a harsh drunk, when your eyes won't stay where you want them to. I had trouble getting back over Joey's fence. I couldn't remember setting the alarm. I only set it on special days, like Christmas.

I got up. I didn't change out of my pajamas because I wanted to have breakfast in them. It took me some time to pee because it wouldn't come out.

The kitchen was dark, so I opened the shades. The grass in the backyard was starting to brown. An old man with a green mini-tractor used to take care of the lawn every other Tuesday except holidays. The old man's hips hung over the seat, and he drove the mini-tractor around and around the backyard and did something right, because the grass was green then.

In the kitchen, I met up with the sight of the houselady stooped over the dishwasher. Flower print spread over a light bulb.

"Rinse first," she said while she jostled about cups and brought some up onto the counter. "I'm going to have to run most of these all over again."

I hummed and stepped around her for the cereal cupboard. The houselady always bought nutritional cereals, Crackling Oat Bran and Shredded Wheat, full percentages of the US RDA on the sides of their boxes, but Joey always made sure I had a box of Froot Loops or Cookie Crisps. He had been in a house like mine, he told me once, and knew what it was like. I grabbed the Loops and put them down on the counter and went to the refrigerator for milk while plastic clattered behind me.

The calendar on the freezer door had a picture of a girl in a blue bikini standing in a motorboat. She was Hawaiian or Samoan, a Craftsman chainsaw in her grip. Along the bottom of the picture, the chainsaw's blade length, horsepower and retail price. The corner store kept a pile of these calendars for free by the register. A couple of the houselady's magnets held up the corners of the picture—unfurled scrolls, quotations from the Bible written in calligraphy. I was most fond of January, and sometimes I turned the pages back to stare at her for a while. January wore an orange bikini and stood in front of a log cabin as she held up a portable jigsaw. Her tan was close to the color of her bikini, and she looked like Vanna White from *Wheel of Fortune*, but today was the sixteenth of

May, and I didn't want to stare at January with the houselady in the room. There was a thick red X marked over today's date. Nothing else in the sixteenth-of-May box except a waning crescent.

I opened the refrigerator. Next to the two-percent milk was the plastic Tupperware box the houselady used to store muffins or cake or cookies.

"What's today?" I said.

"Tuesday," the houselady said. She put her hands on her lower back as she straightened.

"Okay," I said. "But what's today?" I pointed at the Tupperware, though the refrigerator door blocked her view of the interior.

The houselady stared at me and scrunched her brow. She'd told me her name a few times, but the only name I could remember was Trudy, who was the houselady I had for years and years, an old, old woman who didn't come anymore. This one had only come in a few months ago. "What is it today?" I asked again, and still she stared. Maybe she had a coffee party after her shift.

I heard a piff outside. I went to the sink and pushed my face against the window to see into Joey's backyard next door.

Joey had on his Redskins football helmet as he shot a pellet gun into the apple tree in his backyard. An apple fell, and Joey yelled, "Got another one." He raised the gun in the air. I ran upstairs and changed into my outside clothes. I didn't go out until I was all buttoned up. The houselady called my name, asked when I was going to be back, but if she didn't want to talk, neither did I.

I stepped slowly over the low chicken-wire fence and tried to sneak up on Joey, who was aiming and had his back to me, but he turned before I could grab his shoulders and spook him. Joey had radar. He was a veteran. Korea gave him a scar on his stomach and a red spot on his head and monthly checks large enough for him to live in this house on his own. Joey also couldn't smile with the right side of his face. I knew his house better than I knew mine.

Joey and I met when I bought a creamsicle at the corner store with money the houselady let me have. Joey was coming in the front door as I was going out, and when we bumped I dropped my creamsicle, so Joey took me back inside and bought me another. It was the only ice cream with a stick I ever saw Joey buy—Joey liked ice cream sandwiches. Then he invited me over to his house to watch TV. He bought two bottles of Wild Turkey and we almost finished them that first night together. Joey fell asleep in his TV-watching chair and I watched a late movie about giant ants and couldn't remember later how I got home.

"Good morning, buddy." Joey put the Redskins helmet on my head, gave me his pellet gun and ran back inside. There were fallen apples, whole and broken, in the grass under the tree. I cocked a pellet and shot at an apple, but the gun was the one with the bad sight. A couple of leaves jerked from the puff of air. I aimed a little to the right of the apple and fired again. I hit the apple up near the stem. I had to hit it two more times before it rocked and fell.

"I got one," I yelled. I shot at more apples and more apples fell. "I got another," I yelled again.

Joey came back outside with his Bears helmet and his new pellet gun. I wasn't a Redskins fan. I liked the new gun, a blue steel pump-action that looked like a genuine .22 Galil as long as you didn't look at it for too long, but I never got to use it. Both Joey and I shot at apples, and apples fell. "Got another one," I yelled. "Got another one, goddamn it," Joey yelled. A bad apple fell onto my head. Juice and apple chunks dripped onto my facemask. I shot at apples until Joey grabbed my gun by the barrel.

"Enough," he said. He took the Bears helmet off, and I laughed. "Helmet head," I called him.

Joey said, "You're up early." He brushed his hair back with his free hand. Then he licked his fingers and palm and brushed at his hair again, but nothing worked. "I thought you were going to sleep later," he said. "How was the movie last night?"

I took off the Redskins helmet and shook off bits of bad apple still stuck to it. "It was a vampire movie," I said. Joey nodded. I brushed my fingers through my hair and Joey laughed.

"I didn't get to shower yet," I said.

I asked Joey what today was and he said, "Tuesday, I think." He went to the back door, picked up an apple basket and threw it to me. I dropped the Redskins helmet and pellet gun in time, but the basket passed between my open hands.

"Yeah, it's Tuesday," Joey said. "The groceries came yesterday, so it must be Tuesday." He picked up the other basket and said, "Pick them up before they get rotten," pointing at the fallen apples in the grass. Joey and I picked up whole and mostly whole apples. Joey said, "Leave the bitty pieces. Give the worms some breakfast."

Joey and I drank gin in the living room while the pies baked. Joey and I hadn't gotten drunk in a couple of weeks, not since he went out to some bars when his check came in. I waited all night for Joey's lights to come on, and Joey had Band-Aids and bruises the next day. He told me he fell and couldn't do too much, so until he felt better, he sat around and didn't drink. We watched TV all day and night, and he didn't drink at all. When Joey did try getting up from his TV-watching chair, he grabbed his ribs and groaned and cursed. But now we were both drinking again and Joey only had one yellow patch left under his eye. Joey looked through the TV schedule, and the apple pies had extra cinnamon in them since some of the apples were a little sour. The living room filled with the smell.

"Damn, Beaver's not on today," Joey said. "There's a telethon on," he said. "You hungry?"

I said, "I didn't have breakfast yet," and I finished my drink. The Gordon's was next to Joey across the room.

Joey said, "So?"

The cinnamon smell bounced around my empty stomach.

The oven timer went off, and Joey got up. "The pies," he said. He took the gin to the kitchen with him, and it took me three tries to get up from the sofa.

Joey put a lot of vanilla ice cream on my second piece of pie. The ice cream helped cover the sour the cinnamon hadn't gotten to. "You're eating slow," he said.

"Is it a holiday today?" That red X.

Joey stabbed around his piece of pie with a fork. He said, "There's a pellet in here."

"I tried to get them all out," I said.

"Well, you missed a couple." Joey wouldn't look at me.

"You only found one," I said.

"Bit one before," Joey said. "I didn't tell you right then because you were drinking."

"Sorry," I said. "I tried," I said.

"You have to fork through to find the pellets."

"Sorry," I said. "It's real easy to do," Joey said, and I said, "Sorry."

"The pie is fine besides," Joey said. "Good apples."

"Should be," I said to my plate. "Your recipe."

"What does that mean?" Joey put down his fork.

"Sorry," I said.

Joey said, "Don't worry. It's a happy day for you. Don't worry."

I put down my fork. Happy day.

Joey picked up his fork, and he ate and looked at me again. "Did you watch Beaver last night?" he asked. "Wally had these two girls who wanted to go with him to a dance. Beaver thought he shouldn't take any girls out. 'Girls are yucky,' he said. It was good."

"I think I missed it," I said. "I think I went home."

"Happy birthday," Joey said.

I didn't pick my fork up. My ice cream was melting. I was fifty-eight.

No horror movies that night, but there was a kung-fu movie on Channel 27: *Spikes of Death*. Joey and I watched it and finished off the second bottle of wine he had bought to celebrate my birthday. The pie was gone and it was getting hard to watch the TV. I kept drifting and staring at the blue wall over the sofa. I tapped the arm of the sofa with the hammer Joey had bought me.

"Let me use that hammer sometime," Joey said. "Need to fix the coffee table."

I nodded and stared at that wall.

"Did you see Beaver today?" Joey asked, and I shook my head and told him, "No."

"Shame," Joey said. "Me neither."

I poured the rest of the wine into my glass. A kung fu fighter in the movie went to a wedding, and Joey rubbed his face and sniffled. "I think I'm drunk," he said. "Ever think of getting married?"

"No," I said. "They're yucky." I laughed and didn't know Joey wasn't laughing until I had stopped.

"Ever?" Joey asked.

"How can we?" I said. "I'm fifty-eight."

"There are girls our age," Joey said.

"Yeah, but you know how they are," I said. Maybe the houselady was my age. She only proved my point..

"Yeah," Joey said. I tried really hard to stare at the TV, but I drifted off again, and when I snapped out of it, Joey was tapping his glass against his forehead. The quiet was too much, so I said, "Whaddya say we take the pellet guns, go out and shoot one of Crabby Jones's cats? That ought to get her real pissed." Crabby Jones lived across the street. I looked at Joey and hoped he would remember when Crabby told us to stay the hell away when we went for a walk through her yard one night. She told us she was going to have the police take us away, but Joey's lip quivered, so I told Joey how good the pie was, anything to stop that quiver. I said, "Great recipe. Those pies did have pellets in them, though. God, I must have missed six of them." I slapped my head hard with the heel of my hand and then hit myself again, harder.

"You have to mush through the apple with a fork," Joey said. He moved his hand in the air as though he were

57

mushing through a pile of apple chunks, then he stopped. He said, "They're going to put me back." Joey waved his hands in the air and started crying.

I wanted to go away, maybe to the kitchen to wait until Joey felt better. Joey's TV-watching chair was within reach of the liquor cabinet, but Joey didn't reach for it. He stared at his glass and he coughed one of those sobbing coughs. I wished that I hadn't woken up that morning. Maybe I'd still be falling, which was a scary feeling, but I knew what I was scared of when I fell.

Joey put down his wineglass and didn't stop crying. Tears dripped into the lines on his face. He looked tired and old, like someone who had been through a lot, and it made me feel old, too. Even though the shades were down, I wondered how we would look if someone came by and saw us. I wondered if we looked like an old Wally and the Beaver, with Wally crying.

"Maybe you want to watch the news?" I asked.

Joey asked why. I could barely hear him.

"I don't know," I said. "Maybe something important is happening," I said.

Joey nodded slowly.

I got up from the sofa, but it was like I weighed a ton, my knees about to snap and break. I was close to the TV when an ice-cream commercial came on. A scooper tore up a landscape of rippled chocolate chip mint.

"Ice cream," Joey said. "I want ice cream." He smiled, and he turned to me. His tears hadn't made their way down all of his face yet. They glowed blue with TV light—TV tears.

"It's late," I said. "Maybe we should go to bed." Maybe go home. Maybe I'd call Joey in a week or so if I ever felt like coming over again.

Joey got up and hurried out of the living room. "We're gonna get some ice cream at the corner store," he said as he went. He ran upstairs, talking loud, but I couldn't understand what he said. I wanted to run upstairs too.

I yelled, "Can we get popsicles?"

Joey didn't stop talking. He came downstairs with a handful of money and he said, "We're gonna get some ice cream at the corner store," as if he were saying it for the tenth time.

"Are we gonna eat it here?" I asked Joey, and he said, "We're gonna eat it here." Joey almost fell down, but he caught himself. "We'll get lots," he said. "Enough to last us a few days."

"Can we get popsicles?" I asked. "Cherry, maybe?"

"You don't even have to go home," Joey said, the real Joey. He said, "You can sleep in the extra bed. We'll have ice cream together, you and me."

"I'd settle for orange or strawberry," I said. I walked right behind him, so there would be no chance of losing him.

"The cabinet's full," Joey said as he ran down a checklist in his head. "No worry about that."

"Maybe even creamsicles?" I asked. "Creamsicle, creamsicle, orange creamsicle," I sang, and Joey kept right on thinking like crazy as he walked around the living room. "There's a good movie on tonight," he said. "There's a vampire movie on tonight. There's a weeklong festival. Then we'll get out the guns, and Crabby's cats should be out by then. I'll take the new gun because it still has to be broken in." Out the front door Joey went, and I followed.

Crabby's cat Kramer sat the middle of the street. Joey pointed his finger at the Manx and pulled back his thumb. "Eat pellet, puss," he said. I saw a light in the kitchen to my house.

It wasn't light bulb light, more like firelight, something burning. Candlelight? No matter. I looked down the street at the other blocks, and they looked like paintings, but I figured it was just the fog doing that. Joey laughed, and the laugh almost echoed.

No More, No More (in iambic pentameter)

I Morning

My doctor also says I drink too much. "No more, no more," this doctor orders me.

II Evening to Mourning

The barman points, *Another round?* intoned.

"No more!" I cry; "I'll go," I wail; "I leave."

My guts, they rot with mange and dusty flame. I see my plot—a sole, deserted death.

My barman smirks; I wet my soul with wine.

Falling

In this white space, a dot (a red dot [red not like blood {still a horror, to be sure!}, but like cherry candy {dare I invoke Lifesavers and irony (easy, easy—there is time to be taken, a start to be made, time to set up the importance of this dot)?}, red like wild cherry soda, like all the positive things you can imagine {even the positive things not red (a puffy, overblown beach ball [granted, with only a slice of red], puppies I regret to say, the joys behind various food items [scrambled eggs, pizza with black olives, flounder stuffed with lump crab meat, chicken saagwala {don't forget the papadam}, sushi], music of the highest sort {the conductable works of antiquity}); like the Chinese saying goes, "It's so red, it's purple,' but purple here, with this red dot, would slam down certain sinister implications, despite all my attempts otherwise, for something there is that does not love a red dot {the housewife inside us all—the one with the flowered housecoat} and would find it vile and filthy and a soreness unbearable {woe to him who finds this dot on the carpet!}, no matter how much I may defend it with the philosophies of Feng-Shui masters}, but even if this red dot held the secret to happiness on Earth for ever and ever and an ever, the fact is that this red dot is of unknown composition, and though the dot may resemble a perfect tiny circle, and the red a shade of the juice that suspends maraschino cherries, and though the horror of this red intends to hide under a pleasing facade, the dot burns red and announces its horror despite my best efforts]—a dot most definitely red, and most definitely a dot).

Beside it, another falls…

Textual Notes to a Lost Work

1.   Originally published as "The Mouse Trial" in *Rodent Quarterly* (v3n5), a publication dedicated exclusively to writings about mice: mouse poems, anecdotes about rodents, lab reports, recipes for mouse-inspired delicacies (cheese dips, sauces, ratatouille), reports on any newfound species, and of course hints, advice and insider tips on exterminating the varmints. P.L. DeM. and then editor, Humphrey Burger, met in a bar after DeM. performed a reading there (the reading was actually one not solicited by the establishment, and Burger waved off DeM.'s impending arrest by saying the poet was his guest). Burger was impressed by DeM.'s work and promised publication if the poet agreed to change his title to something more fitting with the *Rodent*'s stated purpose. This relationship was to last many years and create a forum through which DeM. would have most of his early works published, though the titles would be changed later to something more suitable (Q. Knickers, *Pests: DeM. and the Not-Giving-Upness of His Years with* Rodent Quarterly, 1976).

2.   One of the many fish clumped together under the classification of 'sardine'; its head alone is often enjoyed as a delicacy in Korean cuisine.

3.   Lines 8-16 also appear in "Dismembering Bartenders" (*The Thing Hanging at the Back of My Throat*, 1953),

though the angora sweater is replaced by mohair in the later work.

4.　　This line has often been considered the first instance of DeM.'s 'dyslexic technique.' Anagrams have offered many interpretations of this line (from a rousing recapitulation of the Postmodern ethic to a request from its narrator for another helping of tiramisu), but Paul RuPaul (*DeM. as an Exercise in Reader Response, Aristotelian Method and Holding Back the Urgent Need to Pee*, 1964) found evidence of 'dyslexic technique' in a self-published, untitled poem dated ten years earlier (P.L. DeM., *Brown Spittle and Other Poems of No Worth*, 1945(?)).

5.　　Thomas Crapper is credited with inventing the first flushing toilet.

6.　　'To pair winged with straw rather than pipe would have served me better purpose'—P.L. DeM., "Interview with a Rat" (*Rodent Quarterly*, v5n3).

7.　　'Nausea set in by this point'—Ibid.

8.　　This stanza was later used as an epigraph in the essay, "Trees: Self-Organizing Systems of Leaf-Withering and the Purpose of Poetry." This essay was a transcription of a talk given to runners-up in a national search for young talent, and the epigraph was attributed to Samuel Taylor Coleridge. DeM. lamented to his audience after the reading of the stanza: 'You know when to hang up your keyboard when you realize an addicted boob like Samuel T.C. can write a better set of lines when hooked to a hookah and getting head from a stank wench than you can after twenty years of professional training' (P.L. DeM., "Trees: Self-Organizing...": *Works the Bastards Refused to Print in the Selected*, 1968).

9.　　The substance human flesh turns into when allowed to freeze.

10.　The anachronistic nature of this quatrain led Nove McGuirk to theorize that Humphrey Burger commissioned these lines as a word puzzle to stump *Rodent* readers:

> Humphrey Burger may have convinced DeM. not only a change in title but to offer a kind of 'mouse maze' in the work itself; the unusual starting letters of the four lines (V, R, X and N (in that order)), when paired with their 'mirror'

letters (found when the alphabet is basically folded in half so that A is paired with Z, B with Y, and so on) form EICM (in that order), an anagram for the word 'mice,' the central theme of *Rodent Quarterly* (N. McGuirk, *P.L. DeM. and the Method Behind the Slightly Off-Centeredness*, 1958*).

> *McGuirk's only full-length critical publication on DeM., or any other major poet, for that matter; she was removed from her position at the U of M shortly thereafter. This book of criticism is not cited as any reason for her termination.

11.   Long thought a misprint, the 'me' here was restored with its original, authorial intentions when it was revealed by biographer Neville Bloodwart that DeM. was prone to a nervous tic when speaking in the possessive, especially in reference to alcohol. DeM. would squint his left eye and speak from the right side of his mouth, soliciting the nickname 'The Pirate DeM' from his close friends. His would demand 'me rum,' or 'me shot of mescal' (N. Bloodwart, *Epitaph or Epigraph?: The Sad, All-Too-Long Tale of a Miscreant*, 1978).

12.   DeM. offered a revision of this line to his anthologist during the compiling of his Selected Works, but this revision was returned to DeM. shredded quite professionally and tainted with a 'smelly residue' (P.L. DeM., *Works the Bastards Refused to Print in the Selected*, 1968).

13.   Authenticity of this reference is in dispute, since the invention and marketing of Silly Putty did not happen until five years after the final version of this poem.

14.   'Beast' could very likely have been mistaken for the word 'breast': the original draft of the poem for *R.Q.* was written on used paper towel. DeM. himself was loathe to authorize the narrator's 'pocket' as one found on 'the Beast' or 'the Breast' (Bloodwart); both readings have spawned various interpretations (see R. Brick, *Cooking with Sherry: DeM. and His Critics*).

15.   see note 9. Another byproduct of the freezing process.

16.   see note 15.

17.   A mathematical theorem used by numerologists to predict the winners of horse races. Sometimes used in factoring the odds of a cockfight.

18.   The source of this quote is undiscovered, if indeed there is a source at all (see 8). Many critics, however, doubt DeM. was capable of such hypotactic structure (see F.T.D.S.M.L-K.R. Gank, "Who Is This DeM., Anyway?", 1956).

19.   DeM.'s continued affinity for S.T. Coleridge is evident when this line appears as marginalia in DeM.'s book-length poem, *The Growth of Sponge* (1964). This is only one of three marginalia in the entire poem, and is considered by some as an error. DeM. was prone to flashbacks at the point of *Sponge* and sometimes composed work he'd already published years prior (Bloodwort). The erroneous nature of this marginalia is also argued in that the two other instances involve demands upon the reader to reject the work that he is reading:

> Vile! Begone! Away with
> Your entreatment to delve into
> This Scourge! Be kind
> And allow its Passage
> Into Obscurity! (112)

and

> You're still here?!
> Still, you plod Along?!
> End this tyranny! (268)

The marginalia offered through this particular line offers not even a reversal of these condemnations (B. Dickus, *Spam and the Art of DeM.*, 1975).

20. see following.

Hill Giant

Morning—his yawn upsets the very pebbles beneath him as he trudges forth to scrounge. He busts through some fencing and dashes sheep, then two, for breakfast. Villagers run in fright, their main occupation. What choice have they?: their heads come not halfway up his thigh.

Guts and bones and fleece pawed through, morsels devoured, lick smacks that echo. He slings a mostly whole carcass over a shoulder, offal dripping into his chest and back hair, and it's back to the cave with him.

The mate awaits on a pile of rubble. Grunts, growls, an ape-like scream and more, and her breakfast plops like wet moss before her. He cowers back to the opening of the cave and peers up at the sun. So bright. He calls to have the stars back, but nothing listens. He dares enter the cave again only when she has a mouthful of food, when she's busy studying the half-sheep for another strategic bite. She slurps and gulps, she holds her stomach a moment, she growls and has at the sheep again.

The villagers have gathered tools and fire and raised their own hackles with angry words and laments over their loss of livestock. They find him in a field, stripping the branches of an apple tree clean between his teeth.

No one understands each other: he does not like to fight when full of fruit; they are keen on fire and think everything but them fears it. Villagers are thrown into lethal positions, when all they manage is to rake his shins. The torches singe his leg hair; one so lucky as to heat his testicles. He pinches one villager's head until it pops, backhands three from whence they came.

He hates most stepping on the bodies—such unsure footing. Like walking on dunghills. Once, he happens to slip, catches himself on a hand, and the villagers converge and prick at his wrist with their hoes, incur boo-boos with their scythes. Another team has at his ankles with hammers and sticks. Is that one trying to bite him?

Villagers flattened, villagers broken, villagers dashed upon rocks. As they retreat, he gnashes the arm of one between his teeth and sprays bloody spittle and flesh and crushed bone at the fleeing force. The wounded squirm and scream and cry as he picks them up and drops them, higher and higher, until they've stopped moving. The one that lasts the highest he holds aloft reverently to the darkening sky. The body dangles broken limbs between his fingers. A light moan now and then: feeble, hopeless ones.

A good one. He drapes this body over his shoulder as a trophy.

He follows the villagers' tracks for a bit to make sure their retreat is complete—their numbers have diminished greatly, but there is always another swarm out there ready to prick at him at his slightest transgression into lands they consider their own. They spawn like mosquitoes, like cattle; they dig lines in the earth and grow things in unnatural patterns. He swells with anger at them for the effort they made him put in today, and he decides he will crush one of their huts tomorrow and make their women scream and splatter some of those little, helpless babies and scatter their cultivated grain.

His mate will kill him before he ever gets to know that child in her belly—this knowledge burns him in his very genes.

He makes off with two choice victims: plump, bloody and still mostly whole (she likes the bloody ones). His mate snatches these from him and growls him from the cave before she bites into her evening meal. Bones crack between her jaws. As she eats, she looks at him with hatred, with instinctual rage, this child whose kicks literally jolt her and push her about the cave the source of all her distress yet the last thing she'd take it out on.

She's going to crack his head open one day. He hovers at the mouth of the cave, reading all this in her eyes. She's going to bite his face and rip half of it off at one go. This child will feast on his thigh. If he's lucky, he'll be dead when all this happens.

Below, he can see the villagers' squares. Their fields. Their huts gathered in ordered arrays of light. The fires they hold in such high esteem.

The stars are visible. He points his face toward them. How can no one else be crying to the sky on a night like this? When he howls, when he sings his poetry, he can't hear another soul join him.

Curbside Boxes

All the mailboxes in my community are unique: some in color and style, others in shape. The Randstons have a large head that smiles menacingly when the light catches it right. Mail goes in through the part in its hair, out the mouth. Neighborhood kids feed it gravel, leaves, an occasional dead mouse. Theresa and I have taken great care in choosing ours: pink with blue lettering, "Our Home." White bowties encircle the logo.

Just like Sunday evenings, when most everyone in Elm Acres (a convivial development of equidistant duplexes) is either accepting an invitation to dinner or hosting a couple or two himself, the mail is a common denominator in our community. On the way to work, one becomes accustomed to the sight of raised flags, the leg in the air on the Cruzes' crocodile box, as if waiting to be called on. Coming home, one expects those flags lowered, each box bursting with a U of manila envelopes and magazines, letters resting nicely in the bottom curve.

Theresa and I, our problem is the Chevy van with smoky windows that's parked in front of our mailbox. In place of delivering our mail, the mailman has been leaving angry notes on the van's windshield explaining how the presence of vehicles 'parked malapropos' hindered the 'unexpurgated completion of a federally assigned task.' The grammar is exquisite, the font crisp, as if done on a laser printer. Questions? Contact the postmaster.

No one I know has any connection to the van, or at least admits to it. A van like that (Illinois plates, rust around the handles, a Harley-Davidson magnet on the side) becomes an immediate topic of conversation in my community. A van like that blocking mail delivery is an absolute scandal.

On my way home, I can feel people watching me, peeking out from behind curtains, stealing glimpses from the corners of their eyes. Theresa is too embarrassed to talk to anyone or leave the house. When neighbors call, she is curt with them, always with an excuse: a cake is burning, she has dye to wash out, call waiting, something important.

The first two notes were an inconvenience, the third a nuisance. No flyers or junk mail, no free samples. No guaranteed winnings from Publisher's ClearingHouse. Theresa and I spend our evenings in an uneasy quiet. No sales to discuss, no catalog items to point out to each other, nothing to distract us from our situation. We used to read aloud the form letter invitations to try the MasterCard Platinum or join the National Geographic Society as if they were letters from old acquaintances. We felt like everyone else then.

Now, three days' worth of outgoing mail sits on the coffee table before us—bills due, business reply mail, a radio survey —next to three of our mailman's notes, lined side by side. Every now and then Theresa sees somehow they are not yet lined up perfectly and makes adjustments.

When we've had enough of our silence, we watch television, and every now and then we fancy ourselves like the people in that box who can lead normal lives and talk to others about their problems and solve them in thirty minutes or less. It is then that we will hold hands, but for only a few moments, for then our silence grows, things boiling inside me, and we let go of each other before anything else can happen.

*

Day four:

It is the kind of day you can tell is cold from just looking out the window. The very clouds look frozen.

Though there's already a note on the van's windshield when I come home, I remove the pile of outgoing mail with feigned delight, as if the old, stale envelopes in my hand were crisp, glossy flyers with coupons galore, or junk mail making offers in large capital letters that strain the seams of the #10 regular business envelopes with the cellophane-covered front windows

What hangs heavy in my gut, though, is the knowledge that nobody will believe this facade. Martin, our mailman, is of the new breed of mail carriers: systematic, precise, at work six days a week. No sense of justice, no sympathy for keeping the status quo. It is only through our elderly neighbors, who have nothing better to do than wait by their mailboxes at 3:00 p.m. weekdays, 10:00 a.m. Saturdays, that Theresa and I know his name at all. His postal jeep moves robotically through Elm Acres, the tires stopping, it seems, on the very inch they have stopped on every day. Theresa watches from the front window when Martin comes by, but even when we did get mail, she wouldn't dare step out the door until he was at least two boxes past.

I take the note, which is addressed, as always, "Dear Postal Customer," though Theresa wants me to leave it behind to give the van's owner a hint to move. Even approaching the van makes my neck bristle, as though there were someone watching me from behind those dark windows with paintings of Arizona sunsets. Sometimes I think I've caught a whiff of rotting corpses, stowed away until police surveillance cools off.

Pat from the adjoining house has come out, accompanied by the swishing of his pajama bottoms. He is considering the sky, one hand hanging leisurely in the pocket of his bathrobe, as he strolls towards the curb. Pat's other hand keeps a loose leash on Misha, his basenji, who is stalking Pat's ankles as if they were natural enemies.

"Cold," Pat decides aloud when he reaches his barn-shaped mailbox. He rubs his arms and whoops at the chill. Misha yelps at the sudden pulls on her collar. Pat is a pit boss at a casino, third shift. After removing a small pile of letters from his box, he takes a fresh outgoing pile from his robe and inserts them through the barn door. Instead of a flag, a rooster flies.

I shove the note deep, deep into my pocket and turn towards my house. "It was warmer earlier," I say hastily, "when the sun was all the way up."

Pat is already musing over return addresses. "Damn psychic networks," he grumbles. "You call once, and here you are, on every mailing list."

I hum sympathetically, almost on my front porch now.

But then, "Phil?" Pat calls.

I stop and bounce slightly, anxious to be back inside.

"I keep getting stuff for a Tony White. He the guy before me?"

I shrug, though I remember Tony White well, proudly showing off the letters he'd get from the child in a starving land he sponsored. He even carried around the kid's picture —a creature black as night, kneeling on infertile ground, smiling with broken teeth.

Pat shakes his head and pulls back Misha, who is sniffing her way off the curb. "Just that I keep getting porn stuff in his name." He holds up the magazine-sized envelope as he pulls Misha along back towards his own house. "Really savage stuff, too."

I watch as Pat puts a couple envelopes between his teeth, then folds the porn mail into his robe pocket. Who would have thought? A normal man, Tony White. A young bank executive, dating a tall, blond woman his age who wore long-sleeve business outfits with scarves, sometimes turtleneck aerobic wear, always something up to the wrists and chin. I can't help rethinking now what I once thought were innocuous, playful squeals coming through the adjoining wall of our duplex. What images transpired late at night as his living room windows flickered television blue?

*

Theresa is in the kitchen, clearly disappointed. She's using both hands to drink her coffee. I hold out the fourth note for our collection, though I can't imagine why she'd want to see it.

"Is he *allowed* to just not deliver our mail?" She puts her Garfield mug on the counter, brings her fingers to her temples. "Can he just go back to headquarters, or wherever, drop off our mail and tell them, 'Sorry, that van's still there'?"

I want to tell her he can't, though I'm not sure, but then an even worse thought hits me: Martin at home, feet up before a TV, paging through my Sharper Image catalog, checking out the balance on the Visa Gold, steaming off Bugs Bunny stamps for his collection (he has to be something like this— no one can be that precise and lifeless). But Theresa's hands are nervous already, moving between her forehead and the coffee. She needs practical advice, directing toward a course of action, not more trouble, and certainly no stories about how the former neighbor we had over for dinner on occasion, the one who reciprocated, was receiving mail about group sex, sodomy, maybe worse.

"Can a pilot," I suggest, "fly to Paris and not land because he doesn't like the runway he's assigned?"

"Exactly." Theresa makes a fist and feigns banging it on the counter.

"Can he just fly back and tell them, 'Sorry'?"

In the end, she doesn't strike; she lays her fist quietly on the Formica, as though she were setting down someone else's kitten, then picks up her mug again thoughtfully.

After a moment, she nods in resolution, her bob swinging momentarily into her face. She says, "Complain to the post office," then, of course, turns to me, as if we have never discussed this before. I thought she understood the embarrassment of it, the vulnerability of making an announcement like this before the whole post office, regardless that the post office is closed by the time I'm off work. It is for the same reason that I leave our mail to be picked up by Martin and don't drop it off in any pedestrian, public box: around here things are not done that way.

I know she's only nervous and desperate. House-bound for four days now, she doesn't bother changing out of her bathrobe anymore, but still I get defensive when she reminds me that I'm off Saturdays and I have nothing better to do anyway, so I tell her that Pat saw me taking the latest note off the van and even commented on our predicament, though he didn't, but I can't help myself. I enjoy her shock, the way the mug falters in her grip, threatening to send coffee and shards of Garfield everywhere, but soon comes the regret, and I go back to how I always feel: knowing my actions never help things, not a phone call, not consulting the best psychiatrists, not touching Theresa's hair, nothing...

"You can't go on weekdays," Theresa reminds me. "We can't go another week without mail! We're good people, aren't we? We look like good people. We're good people." She brings her coffee to her lips—forcefully, it seems, as if she were cutting herself off.

I grimace and shrug, helplessly.

Theresa has given up on us ever being part of the community again. Saturday morning, I stood by our mailbox and waved to Martin as he approached. I held up a handful of outgoing mail, fanned out Japanese-style, for everyone to see. As Martin left another note under the van's wiper, I called out, "Nice day, eh, Martin?" Theresa thinks I did this because of my drinking, but I denied it. I couldn't even remember how much I drank the night before.

Martin didn't even acknowledge my presence. His movements remained mechanical, unattached, his uniform cap perched exquisitely on his head, but still I kept on, even as he puttered along to the next box. "Nice day, wouldn't you say? Wouldn't you say so, Martin? Did you hear about the Arctic front moving in?" I was screaming by this point, howling. I snatched Martin's latest note, threw it to the ground and stomped it to oblivion.

"Supposed to be *real* cold by *Mon*day, yes *sir*, really *really* cold."

Theresa started crying before I got back to the house. It seemed only natural to grab her arm and yell in her face.

"You wanted me to talk to him. He didn't have much to say, Theresa, what do you think of that, huh? You want me to write him a letter?"

To Theresa, it wasn't the last straw that only the Kakolyrises, the most spurned household in Elm Acres, invited us to Sunday dinner. The last straw was that I accepted.

The invitation was for dinner and drinks, though we start with the latter. Douglas Kakolyris, a contractor with forearms the size of my calves, makes what can be loosely called martinis—Absolut stirred with a vermouth-dipped spoon. Theresa has three. She walks unsteadily, her fingers at her chin, when coming back from the bathroom for the eighth time. She refuses all my assistance, even an inconspicuous hand on the small of her back. We've been fighting like this: I yell at the mailman, she burns my pancakes; I yell at her, she throws away the remote control; I accept the Kakolyrises' invitation (which came, curiously enough, just minutes after the incident with Martin), she refuses to shower. She merely puts on a clean dress and a lot of perfume.

Since the beginning of the evening, Douglas has been on about his latest job, the drywall and 1/4" piping and the goddamn roofers. He grips my shoulder as we sit together on the sofa, as if to make sure I don't run away. Douglas is a huge man, his upper body a wrecking ball with arms. The very weight of his hand makes my shoulder perspire.

Theresa and Lulu, Douglas' wife, take the loveseat. They angle toward each other, their knees almost touching. Lulu is round and Asian and tiny. Her feet dangle. Douglas could hide her from anyone's view.

And before Douglas can continue with his discourse on the techniques of spackle, Theresa blurts out, "There's a van in front of our mailbox, and Phil doesn't know how to do much about it, doesn't know how to do much about anything," and nods to me—round six. "Martin hasn't brought our mail for almost a week."

"A week?" Douglas' great and round and Greek eyes are wide with what must be forced bewilderment. How can they not know? For a moment, I'm suspicious and wonder what else they could want from us.

But it is still good to have someone who actually cares to listen.

"A van?" Lulu is leaning forward now, about to slip off the loveseat. "You could have it towed."

"That might do it." Douglas claps his meaty hand to my shoulder again. He leans in so close I can smell olives. "It's just been sitting there, right? By this time, I think you can assume it's abandoned."

I squirm a bit. "I don't know," I say. I can only imagine men in dirty flannel shirts and baseball caps with various insignia keeping at bay their unkempt hair. They are banging on my front door, screaming, "Where the hell is it? Get out here!"

"We don't know what to do," Theresa continues. "I can't tell you what it's like without mail." She picks up her fourth martini, the one she told Douglas not to make. "You see things around the house you've wanted to forget." She blows me a kiss.

There is good reason why the Kakolyrises are the outcasts of our community. They live among the back lots, where the cheap units are being built. The area is unsightly, with tracks of red dirt and randomly placed stacks of cinder block. Douglas only has any money because of a lawsuit from a bad accident involving a ladder and a trowel. It's his excuse to sit around, tell others what to do and get so enormously fat. Through his white Arrow shirt I can see his scar—a long, lightning-bolt seam along the side of his chest that is pinched and puffy where the rolls of his fat meet.

Lulu is a Korean mail-order bride Douglas bought when his settlement came through. Rumor has it she was a dancer in her native land. Mrs. Dahl who lives down the lane from them claims that Lulu never wears underwear, which causes quite a stir with the neighborhood boys when she steps out on a windy day in her mini-kimono. Korean women, I find, tend to be the least attractive of the Eastern stock, and Lulu proves my point. Her cheeks balloon up under her tiny eyes, and the way her fallen perm flops over her face makes one think of a dark sheep dog. Her thighs threaten to burst her stretch pants. I'm told that on their anniversary she relives her dancing years and inserts rolls of nickels, sticks of gum and bananas into herself for her husband's pleasure. Some say she can chew the gum.

Now Theresa is on the verge of telling them everything about us.

"We have to do something," she says.

Despite the motion it creates, I barely notice the exchange the Kakolyrises pull. Deftly, Douglas rises from the sofa as Lulu lowers herself from her seat. With but one step, Douglas is on the loveseat, and Lulu plops down into the impression left in what must be Douglas' favorite spot next to me. Their movements are smooth and quiet. The springs don't even creak when Douglas sits by my wife, though the imbalance of his bulk forces Theresa to lean in toward him. From another perspective, it might have looked like a dance step: simple, rehearsed, refined, all motion restricted to what was absolutely necessary.

"It would have been nice," Theresa says dreamily. "We could have been a regular family once. We had promise. What went wrong, anyway?" She looks at me, and I burn with shame. How long have we kept this from others? I wonder. How long have Theresa and I forced ourselves silent and tried acting just like everyone else, even inside our own house? Somehow, I'm glad it's been said.

First I notice the look exchanged between the Kakolyrises. A look of acknowledgment, of taking note.

I then notice Douglas' hand on Theresa's knee.

"You should drink that," he says, motioning to Theresa's fourth martini. "It'll get warm."

Theresa works on her martini in tiny gulps. Douglas puts his other hand on her back, and rubs it in tight, tiny circles, as if to coax her on, or ease her nausea.

And only now does it occur to me, so simply that I can hardly believe I never noticed it before: there are no smells of dinner, no sounds of lids shaking from the pressure of simmering liquids underneath. No comforting hum from a ventilating fan.

"So have to talked to Martin?" Lulu asks. "Maybe there's an arrangement you can make. Have you gone to the post office?"

I frown thoughtfully, but again I can feel the anger rising in me, the need to lash out. Theresa's lips are still on her martini, and I find it a prime opportunity to strike back at her. I tell all, proudly and with volume, about Tony White, the very Tony White who used to live next door to Theresa and me. I add terms like 'pederast,' 'bestiality' and 'snuff films' for effect, though as far as I can tell, Tony White might have been good friends with the Kakolyrises. Maybe they swapped videos on occasion.

Theresa looks at me with some surprise, but what really hits me is the way the Kakolyrises laugh. Douglas even shakes his head, saying, "And I thought I knew it all."

Elm Acres then opens up to me as if a multitude of car bombs suddenly blew off the front of every duplex. Tony White: A mild-mannered-looking bank administrator who paid his bills, got his mail, drove a nice car. So what if the images he played on TV late at night were less than seemly, less than legal? So what if he did things with his girlfriend so that in the high heat of summer she wore scarves and long sleeve jackets? All that mattered to anyone was that he went to work every day, got his mail and showed us what we wanted to see. I take in a deep breath with my discovery, and the air feels good.

Then Lulu puts her hand on mine and, looking into my eyes, assures me, "The van will move itself."

This is all I wanted to hear for a while, but now I need more, much more, and Lulu seems to know this and responds:

"It will all be taken care of tomorrow, or the day after. Soon enough that you won't have to do a thing about it." She raises her hand to my cheek and gives me an adoring pat. "No one's going to look at you strange anymore. You can do all you are doing right now, and no one is going to care, because Martin is going to stop by your house six days a week, just like everyone else, and that will be that."

"Do you think so?" My voice is barely a whisper, it cracks so.

Lulu gets up and goes into the kitchen.

"Finish your beer," she calls when there.

There is a silence as I gulp down the rest of my Heineken. There we are, Theresa, Douglas and me, staring straight ahead of each other, eyes not meeting, our glasses empty, the drapes all shut. In this moment I love Theresa fiercely, so much I want to cry out about it, but I know we will have plenty of time together ourselves.

Then Douglas suggests, "Lulu may need a hand with that next round of drinks," and I comply. Almost as soon as I am out of the room, I notice a great stillness behind me. It is stillness free of tension—a great releasing—interrupted only by the occasional sound of something wet.

Lulu is leaning on the sink, wiping off a drinking glass. By impulse alone, I come up behind her and put my hands on her hips. I rub up and down the polyester from the elastic waistband to the initial bulge of her thighs. She smells sour this close; her hair reeks of activator.

"Not so hard," she says. "I'll break a glass," but I can't stop, and I dare to bring my hands higher, even to the flap where her breasts begin.

Without rushing, she puts down the glass and turns to face me. Her mouth is soft and wet and tastes remotely metallic. We stop and I pull her to me so I don't have to look in her eyes.

"We're good people," I say. "Theresa and me."

"Yes," Lulu says. The side of her mouth is pressed against my chest.

"We're still going to shun you," I tell her, "just like everyone else. We're going to spread stories about you and make fun of you and make sure everyone else knows we're doing that."

"Of course," Lulu says as she touches that part of me no one's reached in years. "Come over whenever you like."

The Smart Bomb

Glasses perched atop my explosive warhead, I fold the morning paper over itself and await my morning brisket to reheat. I wish ill things upon this toaster oven with its sluggish nature, its lack of even the slightest sophistication. Still, I will not have a microwave in its place—such silly things, the way they hum and buzz a façade of disaster while emitting only a minimal level of curies. Roaches crawled about inside the door of the microwave I once had (aptly named Norman). They thrived on those noisy little rays; they sprouted new legs and growths and clambered happy as you will when the interior light came on.

The ones in lab coats, who mill about in the crawlspace just outside my window, survey me through the devices taped-up in every niche of my little home. They interrogate my discarded orange rinds with microscopes for the residue of government secrets. They document my every move (07:45:38.2: removes glass, subsequently rubs eye; 07:45:43.1: looks down approx. 4.7 cm to left of left leg to linoleum floor [a spot there from last night's gravy?]). Their proboscis clack with delicious regularity when I make the slightest move contrary to their computerized itinerary.

The news is the same every day—hell, hand baskets, etc. I am convinced that newspapers recycle not only the same stories of disaster but the same pictures too, altered using micro bit technology. The scowls and looks of despair are indistinguishable from all the other visages of victims I've seen in my day.

Little more to do than await the completion of the brisket while I gaze out the window. A fine view—I look out onto the steel box that encases my abode. The lab-coated ones wriggle along with their gadgets of measurement and detection. When they peek through my window, they don plastic eyeglass frames attached to rubber noses and bushy mustaches. Either they don't want me to recognize them when I get out of here (and get out of here I must, eventually —what good is imprisonment without any hope of release?) or the noses are some kind of olfactory enhancement device.

In any case, they're taking notes.

Every day also is a visit from Dr. Corn—a nice man with a nice name, though prone to excessive questioning. His arrival is always prefaced by a communal buzz from the lab coated ones. They scatter from sight when Dr. Corn opens the door, already donned in an eyeglass/nose/mustache apparatus. While he sets up the chessboard, he pushes the apparatus back against his face and wiggles the temples.

"They haven't made a custom set for you yet?" I sit back and cross my arms the best I can over my cylindrical chest.

"Always standard issue," replies Dr. Corn. Self-consciously, he pushes on the end of his nose.

"I could probably take a stab at it," I say. As small and scrawny as my hands are—not designed for any kind of heavy manual labor, apparently—they are quite useful for glasses. Instinctually, I seem to know that I would be good at opening small doors, letting myself in through relatively small hatches, disengaging alarms.

"That would be wonderful," Dr. Corn says, a slight smile as he studies the board, though a move hasn't been made yet, "but I'm afraid I'd never find the same pair again." He adds, "They pile them all into a bin we're supposed to take from on our way in," then immediately looks about in a worrisome manner, as though he might have revealed more than he was supposed to.

The phone rings. I am hesitant to answer. Always it is some task they want me to resolve, or a voice quiz they want me to respond to.

But since Dr. Corn is here, I comply and pick up. A screech of data commands me:

> *ASSESS AND TRANSFER GRADED SIMULATION IN ORDER OF SECURITY NECESSITY THE FOLLOWING ITEMS: * F-22 modeling/simulation and test concept development * Joint Advanced Distributed Simulation (JADS) Joint Test (JT) support * Electronic Combat (EC) OT&E test concept assessment and development support for B-1 DSUP, F-22, B-2, and F-15 TEWS * Nuclear survivability support for MILSTAR and Global Positioning System * B-2 Data Reduction and Analysis System (DRAS) development and implementation * Automated Software Evaluation Tool Set (ASETS) development and implementation * Air Force Operational and Logistics Information Systems (IS) test planning and execution support * Cheyenne Mountain Upgrade (CMU) OT&E planning and execution*

Just to get back to the game, I screech back the proper order and assessments. Then, as always, comes the series of equations, all 163,482 of them, asked in that same monotone, the long sequence of stuttering tones with which I answer in kind in nanoseconds flat.

"Most adequate," says Dr. Corn. He moves a pawn, to his misfortune. I see victory in 36 moves.

I begin my assault and move a knight. "A wonder how they forget all that so often," I say. I wonder for a moment, as Dr. Corn makes his next, predictable move, if I should offer the poor man some sympathy, a chance to extend the game a bit further for fun's sake, but this idea is consumed immediately by a series of fail-safes and lockouts.

I will beat Dr. Corn in 34 moves. I position a pawn. Now 33.

Dr. Corn advances a bishop. 32. "They forget nothing, Beauregard, my son" (such an endearing term, this, and it gives me pause). "They are merely testing you." 31.

"And why do they continue to test me..." 30... "when I get it all right every time?" 29. 28. 27. 26, 25. 24. 23. This must be a good question to keep him preoccupied so long. He takes a moment to choose his words before he makes a studied, brilliant defensive structure of pawns—brilliant, though futile. 22.

"They must know that you can give the information in a moment's notice," he says. 21. He makes his move (20) with prideful deliberation. 19. "They must know that at any time, any given moment, all your circuits are intact and ready to carry out your orders." There is a hint of futility now, and now we're down to 18. Now 17. It must be tough for him to keep a raised chin as I bang out moves that counter his thoughtful constructions.

He ponders again. 16. 15, now. He deliberates before 14, his finger lingering on the top of his poor, doomed knight's head for a good, full breath before lifting it. No more knight: 13.

"But there is nothing to forget," I offer. "My memory sits in one place at all times, in the corner of my sight, it seems, useless until I'm given orders to retrieve it, and then it rolls out by no will of my own, a stream I can only sit back and watch as it flows exactly as it has every time before. I can't see where any errors would occur in such a system." 12, 11. Dr. Corn shakes his head—he's drawn himself far too much into this game. Like the other times I beat him decisively, he is taking this game all too personally. Perhaps what bothers him is that I hold no respect for him as an adversary.

"We must be sure, Beauregard," he says, studying the board for some hope of escape. The only one he has is the only one I allow. 10 and 9.

"You don't test the toaster oven," I accuse. "Damn thing. I'm nowhere near a brisket right now, and I starve."

"Patience, patience." Dr. Corn is far from consoling. 8, 7.

They have no power over me. This realization is clear and shuddering. A million circuits become available to me, protocols and sequences the uniformed ones and Dr. Corn hoped I'd never see. All the same, I can understand their fear, understand their reasons for holding so much back, all this power I can feel brimming inside of me. I pity them.

Dr. Corn cannot have seen the change in me. He sways not an inch from his posture of near-defeat-but-not-giving-up. What an image it will be to have burned into my memory. 6, with 5 right behind.

"All in due time," Dr. Corn mutters.

He has no idea.

4, 3.

Tell Everything

The old man, my grandfather: smiling the way he always did, his hat atilt on his unnaturally bald head, his stinking excuse for a leg stinking up the room the way it always did; his cane shaking in his grip as it always did.

This is not all…

"My boy," he said (I swear these are the exact words) as he spread out a hand in way of invitation, as if motioning to sit (O, had there only been a seat!).

"My boy," he said, trying to be kindly, but achieving only an old-man-who's-a-stranger kindly, "my boy my boy my boy." Such a greeting by other elders accompanied a ritual fishing in the pockets for loose change, but he offered only an outstretched, unclenched hand, limp and erect both, like rotten melon rind. "My boy my boy my dear sweet Walter."

I am offered up, prodded forward by the parental ones, my thighs announcing their fat by way of the skeeving together of the shorts clad about them. I approach the old hand groping for me; I notice now the odor of pickle on his breath.

I swear I am telling the whole thing as it happened, front to end, sparing no detail. My instructions are clear, my aim true.

His cane in the right hand, his left hand outstretched. (I've considered the reverse—cane in the left, the right meandering toward me—but I am certain that things were this way.) "My boy my boy," he said, "my boy my boy. My boy my boy my dear sweet Walter." He was not repeating himself—this is recap to keep hold on the moment for full disclosure, a pause if you will, the smelly leg and the cane and the shorts around fat legs and the pickle far from everything I need to tell, and before I go on the moment must be fully assessed, evaluated, deciphered, for there is no going on without that...

No, no going on at all.

So here we are: "My boy my boy my boy my boy. My boy my boy my dear sweet Walter." Please notice the punctuation ascribed, the suggestion of cadence—the placement of the period was by far the most agonizing part.

He smelled thus: tumor, pickle, hospital antiseptic, spoiled aftershave. His cane shook, even as he tried to hold it still, both hands (clenched and un) desperate with their affected shaking. The vinyl beneath him creaked flatulently as he leaned forward to float his shaking paw into my vision with horror movie clarity.

All this, mind you, still inside that moment. All this, and the parental hand prodding pushing me on, pushing me by the left shoulder blade (the left one most assuredly—I can feel it even now) through my slightly sweaty cotton top, I cannot tell you what color no matter how hard I try to remember...I'm doing my best.

"My boy my boy," etc., his hands shaking, one reaching for me, his smell all the aforementioned and something else, as if the coffin were already around him. The coffin, and the mothball effervescence of funeral parlor carpeting.

That smell, those mothballs were there, they were there—I can't express this point clearly enough.

But it's in the hand, I tell you, all in the hand. This story is nowhere near telling you what I need it to unless I make clear to you that hand...

Democritus' Atom

Guil: There must have been a moment, at the beginning,
where we could have said—no. But somehow we missed it.
—Tom Stoppard, *Rosencrantz & Guildenstern Are Dead*

We made bets. Innocent ones at first, silly things a man and woman just starting to test the range of possibility try on each other. Wagers fought in riddles: *put me in a bucket and I make it lighter*, Sphinx-like stuff. The befuddled had to cook the befuddler dinner. The confounded ironed the confounder's weekend wash. With familiarity came more forward wagers: loser goes down on winner and gets no reciprocation; loser is winner's naked butler for the day; loser masturbates while singing aloud "Be Kind to Your Web-Footed Friends"—an image of her I didn't easily forget.

Then she won, over and over, until I couldn't even think of challenging riddles anymore. She, on the other hand, seemed to have a storehouse of nasty riddles to pair with the cruelest wagers for my weakest moments.

The unwritable sentence, for instance.

"Understood: to, too and two." She demonstrated on the legal pad I was to use for my answer. "Write me this sentence," which she did not demonstrate on the legal pad: 'There are three *tü*'s in the English language.' No restructuring, no revision."

She sat before me to display the lack of underwear beneath her stylish, professional skirt. By this time, I had licked her shoes clean. I had wiped her ass, collected a week's worth of piss in a gallon jug which I then had to chug from. Fear of yet another failure was already distracting enough, but now there was also her pussy, a crevasse my penis hadn't traversed for a month now.

Also distracting was the fact that I still had hopes of beating her again. I had a list of things I was going to do to her upon my next successful wager. What joy to spread her across my lap, the short-lived ripples on her unyielding posterior rolling out from under my hand, she slurping down a bucket of mashed tofu through a gag ball, the application of which she would have to beg for. Even a straight-up fuck, a heated shag on the hardwood floor, would have been torture to her, especially if I were the one on top.

I took frantically to writing, my hope fueled by the smell of her vagina, wetting I was sure at the spectacle of my desperation.

There are three to's...

She ripped the sheet from the legal pad upon which I slaved. "Wrong!" she screamed with obvious delight.

There are 3 2's...

"Ridiculous! Inane!" This torn sheet fell heavily, crumbled out of shape by her strong, harsh hands.

There are
There are
There are

The blank spaces glared at me, taunted me, sucked all words from my mind.

"Assume the position," she said.

I had long lost the will to even quibble with her orders when I lost. I lay back as she squatted over me and hiked up her skirt so I couldn't help but see the payment I owed her.

"Open wide, lemming," she said, "it's suppertime..."

...no...this is not it...this goes on too long...summarize succinctly...

*

This is to tell where things went bad with us ('her and me' she would have preferred it—even now, how her orders haunt me!), thus to document the turning point, the definitive, concise moment that effected the lowly state our relationship was to become, at least for me...

"I am," was all I could offer. It seemed like a good answer, but she only laughed and spun in her leather desk chair that was so amenable to spinning.

"Dope," she sung out, "numskull, goon."

"'I am' is three letters," I said in way of defense. "There is no shorter going."

She tapped a clothespin against her teeth with intellectual delight and savage anticipation. "Half-wit. Critic. Stop being so literal." She licked her lips in her sumptuous way and leaned toward me. That smell (her hair), the way her double-breasted jacket held onto the curves in her torso...

She took me through the grammar lesson again: the English language, the sentence in its most legal terms, its two basic criterion: 1). a kernel (subject and verb) and 2). a complete thought. That was it. That was all. The riddle was to pare everything down to its most basic element within given parameters, cutting down to Democritus' atom. She summed up thusly:

"So take me a letter shorter, chimp."

Nervous, I said, "I'm."

Oh, she laughed. She sat before me—I remained standing (a position of power, you'd think), yet I felt cuckolded, castrated, my genitals speared upon the tips of her press-on nails.

"Same thing, weasel," she said. She clenched her fist as though she knew where I was imagining my privates and crushed them into nothing.

"We continue, dolt," she said. The way she held the clothespin, she could have been holding a horsewhip...

...not here...not here...oh god not here...

Ah, the days when I still won. She once had to ask the cashier of a video rental store, "Do you carry *Butt-Plugged*

Mega-Racks 4?" with at least three people in line behind her. Once she had to carry my coattails and sing my praises as we went food shopping. Once, I ate dinner from a plate balanced on her back. Once, she had to call random numbers in the phone book while I boffed her from behind and rave to whoever answered (including voicemail) of her 'grand stallion Scaramouche.'

The two-letter sentence was my first big loss.

"In the imperative," she explained as she waved the clothespin like a pointer at nothing, "the subject, 'you,' is understood. I don't have to say 'you' when I say, 'Get out,' or, 'Put that down...'"

(Oh, how she loved the imperative: "Get on your knees"; "Spread those cheeks"; the dreaded, dreaded "Open wide.")

"But 'Go'?" I asked.

"'Go.' That's all. That's it. You lose," she said and locked her lips in victory.

There was no argument in my defense. I had had my share of wins, then. I pulled down my pants so she could collect.

It was the first time I saw her excitement at my flaccidity. She patted it and poked at it and flopped it back and forth. She giggled and commented, "What a strange thing it is." At the slightest hint of arousal, she rapped it sharply with the clothespin to quell it again. She even held it up and peered down it as though through a telescope.

Then, in a quick motion I took then as a desire to just get it over with quick, she held it in place and snapped the clothespin shut over the very tip.

Even after my groan and near inability to remain standing, she flicked it by the clothespin a couple of times and checked her watch. "Just a few more seconds; almost there, darling. Boy is that thing turning red."

This carried me through the next few wagers, the idea that she never really wanted to do these things herself, but was simply getting carried away with the game...

...but this is not enough...this fails to satisfy...there must be a moment more concise....shorter...more to the point...

*

She wouldn't hear argument, especially if it was to afford my first win in months.

"A one-letter sentence?" She was back in her office chair, her throne, the stance she preferred for our little games. "No way in hell, shit-breath."

My argument: "Say we have an action we are either unable or without inclination at present to name, due either to a lack of vocabulary, or say because we simply want to extend a simple mystery, an action not to be revealed at present for reasons also to be revealed in the future." How odd it was to make my case in this fashion: dried dog turds hanging from holes in my ears she herself had pierced in a most unsanitary fashion; holding aloft the dildo she had me acquire from a gay porn shop; my gaze cast down dutifully at her feet.

"Is this unknown action to be permanently obfuscated, or is its uncertainty merely temporary?" Her feet clenched in their inquisitory way.

"Temporary, of course, but until..."

"Hold on, bucko—time to say the words."

I closed my eyes and said the words: "Dildo, dildo, for up my fan,/Will you thrill like Steely Dan?"

"Good boy," she said. "Continue."

"Yes, my liege. Thank you, my liege." I nodded the dildo in reverence. "As I said, temporary of course, but until its unknownness is lifted, its term of uncertainty is most certainly in a kind of permanence, especially if, for any reason, the solution of the variable should never be found."

Her feet waited with little patience for me to finish.

"So let's call this unknown action Action X. X is by no means the only variable we can apply. Action G would be just as acceptable a name, or action M, as in 'to M,' or, 'I Med today.' He, she, it Ms. 'Ming along on a sunny day' and such."

"Finish your spiel soon," she warned. "Must I remind you that that particular dildo is still a virgin?"

"Ergo...ergo...ergo," I said, vying for time to reverse months of cumulative wagers that had brought me to this state, "if we can thus accept the notion of verb M, expressed as such, then of course the imperative form, ersatz, must be..."

She halted my speech with a simple nod of her big toe and produced the now-near-empty jar of petroleum jelly (the last time she was going to afford me this luxury, to be exact).

"If I follow you then," she said, lovingly spreading the jelly in a thick manner over her pointer and middle fingers. "If, say, verb M were a catch-verb comprising wholly a request involving your need to be sodomized by the dildo you hold aloft, making 'to M' mean simply 'to ram that plastic cock up my fudge hole'..."

I needed no more cueing. I turned around and bent over, my arms behind my back to offer up the spear to impale me by.

"...the imperative of said verb, of course—that is, your demand for me to perform this invasive procedure upon you —would be, then, what? How would you say something like that, eh?"

My whole body was in constriction. I couldn't say a thing. This was supposed to by my victory, I kept telling myself.

"Say it," she said. She had the instrument now. I could hear her coating it, those wet, lip-smacking sounds.

I had no resistance to her anymore. I could feel the word coming...

Poor Tree

I lived outside when I was a young man. One night after some rain, I walked around and around and around a park (who knows where, who cares?), and I decided finally to light a fire. I chose a small, dead tree. One, I had only a few matches and it seemed the easiest to set. Two, a poor, bald, shrunken tree on fire would make little difference to anybody.

I stooped, struck one match and held it under the lowest of the poor tree's branches. I burned the match all the way to my fingertips before I dropped it into damp soil. The branch showed nothing but a little blackening, but that could have been the shadows and the night. I took a chance and struck two matches, half my remaining supply. This time, the branch let off a little smoke of its own.

The man must have come up the path behind me and regarded me for a while since I never heard him until he spoke. Maybe he'd been there from the start.

"You need a longer-lasting flame," he said. "Try lighting up the book itself." He had on a topcoat and a bowler. His face was in shadow, but he held his hands in a helpful affect.

The matches were from a bar that wouldn't let me in anymore. I used to sit in front of some mixed nuts, get warm and not buy anything. The cover was green with an Irish name in white lettering. White firework explosions gave off a spirit of camaraderie, even with people you don't know. I tore off a single match and used it to light up the whole thing.

When the cover caught, I held the burning matchbook under the branch I'd been working on. It caught quickly. The flame was small at first, but it swelled as it moved up the branch to the pathetic excuse for a trunk. Since I still had a good flame on my hands, I lit a branch on the other side.

"That's it," the man said. "It's good and going now." My sentiments exactly.

"The book will burn out in the soil," he said. I dropped the nearly spent matchbook into the damp soil, where it burned itself out.

"Now we have a fire," the man said.

I straightened and backed up until I was next to the man. We watched the fire. The flame moved onto the skinny upper branches. Not even a dead leaf for the fire to curl. Poor tree. Spring had just started, and this tree wouldn't have stood a chance.

"It's best," the man said. He reached behind me and gripped my far shoulder. As the fire picked up, moving onto the trunk that wouldn't have passed for a branch on a respectable tree, the man and I found ourselves in some brighter light. I didn't turn to see his face because I knew what I'd find: wrinkles, a sagging face, gray bushy eyebrows, weight from being on this earth for so long. "Some wouldn't have even considered a thing like that as kindling," the old man said.

"Makes for a goodly amount of fire," I said, "a poor dead thing like that. At least for a little while." The man's hand on my shoulder felt odd and comforting both. The heat from the fire pushed through the warm spring air onto my hands and face.

The man said, "Yep," but probably not in response to me.

The poor tree couldn't stand up to the flame for very long. It fell apart, burnt piece by burnt piece, into the soil. There, the pieces smoked and glowed. A prettier sight than the actual flame.

"There it goes," the man said.

The smoke became gray streaks, ghost-like in the night air. Soon, the whole tree was a jigsaw of glowing fragments in the mulch. The stump stood like a cigar planted in the soil. How long could embers glow like that? The damp soil seemed to be overcoming them already.

"That was something," the old man said, the sentiment I disagreed with. I frowned and he squeezed my shoulder. "Come on, boy," he said, "let's go get a drink." Another disagreement, though this old man dressed like someone who could buy me a lot of drinks.

"Go on, pops," I said.

He went on. He walked with his hands in his coat pockets. He looked around as though he had found a new appreciation for the night. Just before he could disappear from my sight, sirens sounded in the distance. He stopped and turned to me, his face in shadow once again.

"Those might be for us," he said. "Maybe we should both go on." It was good advice, and maybe now I would have taken it and played it safe. But I was a young man then, and I kept watching the embers. Amazing: half of them were out already.

"You hear me, boy?" the man called. "You going to let them get you over a sad little tree that had given up the ghost anyway?"

I watched the embers, how they fought on their way out, those last little specks of orange before they got sucked into the dark.

Forecast

Like good people, everything I say I say twice, like good people. Everything I say I say twice.

Let me say this again. (Let me say this again.)

But no. But no, I won't. I won't, for I will go on. For I will go on. I will tell you, tell you of the joy in my life, the joy my life has become. I will tell you. Tell you of the joy in my life. The joy my life has become.

Okay, okay. Not this. Not this time.

Time—that's something to talk about. That is something. To talk about the weather is something to talk about worth listening to. The weather is something to talk about worth listening to. So, the weather. So. The weather.

It's not that I don't want to talk about my life. It's not that.

I don't want to talk. About my life, I have little to say. I have little to say about the weather, either; about the weather, either I am happy or I am disapproving. Doesn't make much difference. I am happy. Or, I am disapproving. Doesn't make much difference if I say much of anything on the subject at all. If I say much of anything on the subject at all, I say, "Nice day." Or, "Yeesh," I say. "Nice day." Or, "Yeesh." What more is there?

What more?

Is there nothing, nothing? Nothing. Nothing worth saying, nothing nothing worth saying. My life? My life? You have it, your answer. You have it. Your answer has been said. Has been said, has been given, has been received, I guess. Has been given. Has been received. I guess there is little else to say. There is little else, too. Say, about the weather. About the weather we will stay. We will stay and we will discuss cold fronts, stationary fronts, wind torque and the like. And we will discuss cold.

Padre

We had the youth gathered for evening snack (bread pudding—donated, on the verge of the inedible) when in came Padre, and of course the whole place went to hell (though we wouldn't go saying anything like that).

Ch'kai plucked raisins from the square in front of him, using his fork for only a moment when we'd remind him to, then plunged his hand right through the dollop of Cool Whip. He extracted a custardy lump and left it on the table, but not once for once mentioning his boyz—that his boyz were coming to get him soon as they put their nines on those Rogues, that we better not see him or his boyz on the street after making him wash and keep shoes on his feet and keep his hands out of his food because he was Bones, he was East Coast. Not once had he promised Adina and Tamarina their names on gold chains and phat sweats in his boyz' colors when his boyz came through, not once threatened us that he and his boyz better not find out what we drive (those of us who could afford a car), because he was warlord for Bones and could do what he wanted. Even if we were just trying to help, we better not cross him once his boyz came or he was going to bitch-slap us. He wasn't even thinking of throwing his unwanted raisins before Padre, collar unbuttoned as always, entered the scene and asked Ch'kai when his boyz were coming to get him, and again we went through Rogues macing his mother, cutting his girl Sabitha's ear, rolling two of his boyz for their rock.

Ch'kai's hands flew into expression. Bread pudding and Cool Whip hit the table and Eishon and Adina and Jennifer, who kept rocking and sucking her thumb, and our plastic dinner Jesus and Yan'Ner and Yan'Ner's baby boy, Oluwatosin, and even us occasionally, all the way against the wall.

"Ch'kai, Ch'kai, Ch'kai," we started, but by now the ruckus was up.

"We must bring the ruckus to all you muthafuckas," Eishon rapped, and there was little we'd be able to do for a while: Adina and Tamarina dug in with their spoons for solid chunks to catapult.

Padre made his rounds, not bothering to brush at the pudding spots clinging to him, raisins in flight. But Padre's name bounced around most of all right now, the delight of children though these were all teenagers. Even under the childish squeals, we had the feeling something more and something more serious had to be coming. Moments like these, we got scared even though we were only out to help these kids and these kids knew it and treated us kindly for the most part, even Ch'kai, but still: when the ruckus was up, it didn't take these kids too much to go too far. These kids had been pushed that far—farther—all their lives.

But then there was Padre, the high school dropout who lived in the subway for a year.

Padre, with his rap sheet—breaking and entering, fencing stolen goods, forgery.

Padre, patting heads, squeezing shoulders and addressing everyone warmly, personally and by name as though he'd known them all for years, though we could rarely keep track of a kid more than a couple months. We wondered sometimes if Padre got scared too, but he wouldn't show it if he did. He'd had kids rip him off, trash his house—one even stabbed him—but still he drove the van and nabbed kids off the street away from their dealers and pimps and addict friends & relatives and stepfathers and mothers' boyfriends (Jennifer's made her go down on him so often she still couldn't look at a hot dog without screaming). Padre brought them to us, who gave sanctuary—a bed, three square meals a day and an evening snack—and we got them to take showers, brush their hair, show them how to care for their babies (so many with babies), and we cleaned their scars, cleaned their scars, any scars, any way we could, but still these kids could scare us.

Padre even touched Darwin, large and dark as night and just as cold and scarred in every way possible, and Darwin nodded his head so slightly he might not have been doing it at all and it was just us thinking, just for a moment, that maybe someone could get through to him.

Padre took Oluwatosin, five months old, and smiled at him and made him smile before giving him back to Yan'Ner and then touching Yan'Ner's four-month swollen belly lovingly.

His eyes closed.

And we knew what for, for it was as clear and pure to us as though we were doing it ourselves (and we were): sending a blessing through the mother's ugly but donated flower print dress (made, in all honesty, for someone at least thirty years older) and through her swollen flesh and womb. It was a blessing for knowledge, that this child know of all the ones who have gone back to the needles & pipes and the alleyways and the cold, back to street corners, back to their gangs, their boyfriends who are still going to drink and drug and hit them and knock them up and take no responsibility for it any of it, back to old, liquor-reeking queens for maybe just a bed for the night and stale English muffins in the morning, but more likely for more smack, more rock, more blow, more crank. A blessing for this child to move beyond all that and to help lead the others up and out of where they were now, and we were going to keep helping, damn it. We let Padre remind us to keep touching and blessing and feeding and giving all we got and closing our eyes and wishing hard, wishing so damn hard.

Jennifer took her thumb out only long enough to smile, her teeth pushing outward from nineteen years of this habit, and called out, "Padre," without making eye contact, never making eye contact, but at least the smile was genuine.

The Way of It

The old man snatches the bowl from me as though it were a glass heirloom in the hands of an idiot manchild. Once he's hunkered over his dinner of oatmeal and dates and has a firm grip on his spoon, he grumbles, "About time, doofus."

I return to the kitchenette and run the hot water. While I scrub the pot in the tiny sink, the old man inches a spoonful of oatmeal towards his mouth. "Smells like you stirred this swill with your dick," he says. He tongues a clump of date and rifles displeasure in my direction. I continue to scrub. The paneling inside the trailer glows orange in the near-dusk.

For fifteen years, I have trained to kill the old man. I am good with a knife, and I can ooze my way through a dark room, but there is a ritual to uphold, the ritual the old man learned from his teacher. Any awkward beast can ambush unsuspecting prey. The truer art is to kill the man who knows you are coming. The old man took twenty-six years to kill his teacher, but I won't need that long. He has grown small in his overstuffed recliner. His surviving clutch of hair, silver as stainless steel, has grown unmanageable and refuses to remain against his scalp. The old man slaps the wad of oatmeal onto his tongue and hums as the spoon comes out clean between his lips.

"Dry," he says, his mouth still full. "We could caulk the windows with this crap."

Three weeks since my last opportunity. The old man sent me outside as usual, and I jogged a circuit through the trailer park while I waited for him to invite me back in. The old man interrogated me about my jog and the methodology of his murder. I answered his questions well enough that he doused the lights. We stalked each other in the dark. I covered my blade to hide my position. I moved on the balls of my feet, my knees bent to silence the floor. But still the old man sniffed me out and struck my hand with the bowl of his iron ladle. My knife clattered to the linoleum.

"Like a camel on roller skates," he said, disappointment souring every word.

Now the old man says, as he brings another spoonful to his mouth, "You need teeth to chew these dates, cow-brain."

Frank corkscrews through a maw in the far corner of the trailer. His black and brown fur is matted with dirt, pine pitch and early evening air. He stretches each leg in turn as he saunters towards the old man. Still smacking his lips and licking his gums, the old man puts the bowl between his knees and pulls a pouch of cat treats from the side pocket of his recliner.

"There, there, there," the old man says as he tears open the pouch. He tsks and throws past Frank. The tabby zeroes in on the tumbling kibble. He swats it dead in its tracks before he eats it. The old man throws this time to the other side of the room. Frank again pounces before the treat loses momentum. The next one is straight at him—Frank scoops it, mid-air, straight to his mouth.

"Good hunter," the old man murmurs. "A natural, you." Whenever Frank brings in a kill—a baby rabbit, say, or a vole —the old man digs his fingertips into Frank's fur as though trying to loosen something. He tells him, "At least something around here knows how to kill."

This humiliation and indignity are all part of my training. Not only must I be able to pierce the same hollow in the paneling with my knife from across the trailer, not only must

I rehearse the insertion of my blade into the base of the old man's skull for a quick and respectful kill, but I must wash the old man's stained underwear by hand in the tiny sink. I must cook. I must sweep the sheet-thin carpet. Only when I kill the old man and take his place will I give commands and ask questions of my student. Until then, I tend to Frank's litter box. Shop. I crawl through the gravel moat of the old man's trailer and pick out every hint of plant or weed. If the gang of dirty boys, twelve-year-olds who run unattended through the trailer park, kick up the gravel that I have just smoothed out, I quietly repair the damage. The money comes from federal checks addressed to a name the old man says is not his, nor that of his teacher. Who knows how far back our line goes, students killing the old men who trained them and going on to find their own student-assassins.

The old man finishes half of his oatmeal and throws Frank another pinch of treats before he folds up the pouch and puts it in the pocket of his blue luau shirt with orange parrots. He turns to the wall and says, "Be gone, melon-face." His hand lingers by the pocket of his recliner, where he keeps a glass ashtray to throw when I do not respond in time. On my way out, I grab my denim jacket from the spot on the floor where I sleep. I always wear my knife on a shoulder holster.

"Good riddance, turd," the old man calls behind me. When I close the door, the ashtray thumps against it for punctuation. The porch light, which looks like the dismembered torso of the Michelin Man, trembles.

The air is 'tween-season, but sunset promises to bring on a deeper chill, so I put on my denim jacket. The remnants of this morning's rain glisten in the grass. A pickup ambles up the hill into the trailer park and passes me, a squad of paint-speckled riders in the bed. The painters stare. They neither wave nor nod because there are rumors about how the old man and I spend our time together. A flock of yardbirds in the road, the smallest still in training pants, part to let the truck through, then the two sides collapse into each other like waves. While I am still buttoning my jacket, the gang of dirty boys, brandishing plastic pistols, ambush the yardbirds and attack without mercy.

I was once a dirty boy myself in this very trailer park. Running outside was a better option than staying home. Even when my mom remembered to buy food, she beat me on the back with table legs and empty liquor bottles. She held my hands over the stove burners for being a little shit. Every now and then, while I do my yard work, I'll see her in a car or truck with a man, sometimes as many as four. Last time, she spat out the window and took a beer can from the shaggy beast next to her.

"Faggot," she yelled as she threw the can at me. "Go get your shit pushed in." I picked up the can and went back to sweeping the front walk. This was last summer, and I haven't seen her since. Maybe she shacked up with one of the men she rode with. Maybe one of them turned out to be the kind of guy whose truck you shouldn't ride in.

The dirty boys turn their sites on me and fire lines of water from their weapons. "Pah-chew, pah-chew, bitch." I raise my sleeve over my face and step out of range. They pursue, so I jog down the hill. The dirty boys stop at the plywood proscenium to the trailer park, and the largest one, the one in the rattiest t-shirt, tells me I *should* run, homo. They all turn back except Andre. Andre claims to be twelve, but he looks no more than nine, so the other boys push him around and call him Gay-dre. His lips are barely big enough to cover his front teeth. He throws some gravel at me. It falls far short.

"Don't come back," Andre says, "until you have my money." Andre likes to pretend that I owe him. I like him to think he has someone to play with, so I look back over my shoulder as though I dread his pursuit. Andre releases a hoarse cry and runs off after the dirty boys.

I've seen Andre bed down on a drop cloth in the abandoned Bonneville that sits one lot over. He hides if I walk by. By the time I was Andre's age, I knew what trash cans were the best to scrounge from, that a pile of pine branches under a water heater was far more comfortable than harsh fabric inside an abandoned vehicle. To pass time between food and sleep, I skipped pebbles on the road and sometimes pegged a groundhog. I ganked bikes and dumped them in the nearby reservoir. When I was thirteen, I broke into trailers for food and money. I stole glass figurines and collectible plates I smashed later when I got bored. I stole a hunting knife, the same knife I use today, and mugged drunks who staggered up from the bar at the bottom of the hill. I impaled dead squirrels and cats and threw them from my blade. When I was fourteen, I crept into bedrooms and held the blade under the noses of sleepers until they woke. I held my blade in place until they sobbed or begged me not to hurt them. Then I pocketed a thing or two and left. One night, I sliced a man's double chin to see what his fat looked like. Another time, I cut a pretty woman along the length of her forearm just to disrupt that pristine stretch of porcelain white. Then I broke into the old man's trailer. I crept towards the rumble of his snoring. When I took out my knife, the old man struck my hand numb. He clocked me on top of the skull, inciting curly-cue flares of spectral light in the dark.

The old man leaned over me and felt up my arms and legs. He muttered, "You're as subtle as a chimp with elephantitis, but I guess you'll have to do." Then he pressed both hands into my chest until I blacked out.

The bar at the bottom of the hill is The Barrelhead: cold beer, warm stools and sandwiches. The chrome handle of its oak door gleams. The hinges swing easily.

The place is near empty. Two local yokels swipe their attention to the TV. I take a seat where I can see up the hill through a raised window. I keep my focus on the old man's porch light. When it goes out, I am to return. The handle of my knife pokes me in the armpit. I order a Miller from the owner, a round man with a form-fitting apron, who puts up a draft and wipes out the ashtray in front of me. I order roast beef. The yokels stare at the owner when he hands my order to the kitchen. They don't like drinking at the same bar as the local queer, but I pay my tabs, so the owner scrunches his mouth to the side and raises his eyebrows at the yokels. The yokels go back to their show.

The old man says our work is too important to distract ourselves with other people, but as the yokels sneak murky looks at me from under the edges of their cap bills, I swallow down the fact that every three or four months, the old man will crawl up behind me while I sleep. Sometimes he yanks down my underwear, but most of the time he rubs up against it. He is too old to get hard anymore, but still he grinds as though he is invading me. He hisses, "Hee! Hee!" He mashes against me until he is too out of breath to continue. Then he goes back to his recliner and never speaks of these episodes. I could slice new mouths on these yokels before they could get their hands up, but I drown the urge in the dregs of my beer.

The kitchen rings up my order. The owner brings my sandwich with extra napkins. He refills my glass. While I eat, I tear confetti-like fragments from the paper plate. The rye bread is crumbly, the meat as tough as a stack of shingles, but I soften each bite with a sip of beer. I put the paltry excuse of a pickle slice up on its end, and it bends like an ocean invertebrate. The yokels risk some quarters on the bowling game behind me. The owner wipes down the spots of nonexistent customers. After I finish my sandwich, I pull a Phillie from the pocket of my denim jacket and light it up.

I have a third beer while I wait for the old man's signal. The bowlers shell out almost three dollars and still can't score a perfect game. They scratch their heads and beards and puzzle at their inability. I know how they feel. The old man sits in a recliner day after day, yet he is still able to best me in the dark. I exhale and watch the smoke as though it might reassure me that tonight I will complete my training. I am at the bottom of my third glass when the light on the old man's trailer goes out.

When I call for my bill, the owner squints and gives me a figure. I leave a mere pittance of a tip. The owner calls out behind me, "Have a better one," as he picks up his money from the bar.

*

I turn up my collar and jog up the hill. Night has delivered its promised cold. The porch light flashes on and off with the old man's impatience, but when I reach the stoop I bounce in place for warmth. If I barge in without invitation, the old man will declare me a failure and remain alive. While I wait, Andre approaches with a broom handle. He is marred with mud and strands of spider web. He smacks his palm with the broom handle. His teeth break out from between his lips.

"Where's my twenty bucks, buster?"

I pat my pockets with horrified energy. "I left it at the bank,"

He points the sharp end of the handle at me. "I'll take it out of your hide," he says. "You owe me a hundred fifty now."

I make motions of distress, a mock gnashing of teeth and rending of garments. "A hundred fifty," I say, "a hundred fifty! Where am I to get a hundred fifty dollars?"

Andre swaggers closer. "Just give me your car," he says, "and we'll call it even."

There is potential to Andre. There is about forty years' difference between the old man and me. I don't know if a twenty year gap is enough to let Andre be my student, but this boy is wiry and would do well with a knife. He can dodge stones pitched at him. I point to the abandoned Bonneville that has served as a pirate ship, a Mars lander and even a tomato juice factory according to who's played in it.

"All yours," I say. "The keys are under the front seat. Take her for a spin."

Andre laughs heartily, almost ape-like, and takes off for the Bonneville.

I rub the sleeves of my denim jacket. Down the hill, The Barrelhead shines like a diamond in a coal bin. From behind the door, the old man calls out, "It's unlocked, oaf." I enter.

The old man holds the ladle in his lap, a banana hanging precariously from his shirt pocket. His silver hair akimbo. Frank is draped along one of the armrests as though he imagines himself on a tree bough.

"You were playing with that child again," the old man says. He looks at his ladle and grins. "You can't find your student until you've killed your teacher, and I can still stove in your skull." He waits until I am on the verge of responding, then says, "Tell me the way of my death. Go through it for me step by step."

"The room is dark," I say. "And I cannot see nor hear you."

"Do you wave about or make noise to see if I will give away my location?"

"I'm on the job," I say. "No reasons to take shortcuts or attract undue attention."

The old man nods and eases back. He takes the banana from his pocket and holds it by the stem as if for comfort. "Proceed." Franks lifts his head to sniff at the fruit.

I go to the window that overlooks the front stoop. I see a shady visage of porch lights and trailers, but mostly I see my reflection, the old man protruding from my head like a tumor. "So I wait in the dark," I say, "to acclimate and steady my breath. I relax, though not so much as to be unprepared."

"Is the darkness an enemy?" the old man asks. "Or does it invite you in?" He peels the banana and holds the naked fruit at arm's length. It may be bait, a promise of reward if I respond well. But maybe he is just preparing to eat it himself.

"The dark is the dark," I say. "Whether you conquer it or not, it is the nature of night to be dark and I must regard it as neither friend nor enemy."

The old man smiles more at the banana than at me as he breaks it. "Half?" I take his offering, and we eat in silence— me with mindful bites, the old man with excitement and relish. The banana is a cloying counterpoint to the Miller and roast beef on dry rye and residue of cigar smoke in my mouth and nose, but the old man will beat me if I show displeasure. When he's finished, the old man slaps his hands together seal-like.

"Ah," he says.

When I stare into my reflection on the window, I can eventually see through it. First I make out the Bonneville, which shakes with whatever game Andre has devised in there.

I examine the neighboring trailers. At first glance they all look the same, but I study each until I find the detail that makes it stand out from the others. This one across the way has vertical blinds and a plastic owl nailed to its roof. The next one over has plastic daisies in its front bed, the kind that spin their heads in the breeze. Two other trailers pulse with the energy of television. One pulses with more frequency, as though someone were asleep on the remote. They all look full, loaded down, resistant to any sudden deluge or twister that may sweep through. The old man's trailer is so spare it could float away like a parade balloon. I may have to bury the old man under the floor to keep my home in place.

I eat the bottom tip of the banana. In the corner of my sight, the old man nods as he counts each pneumatic press of my jaw.

"Thirty," he orders me. "Don't let it slide back before thirty. Even if it's gone to liquid. Then we'll go back to the way of it."

I work towards thirty, the banana more like paste at this point. I will paint these walls when this trailer is finally mine. Also, I will put Frank out on his ass and get myself something part pit bull.

"Chew slowly." The old man claps his feet against each other. "I am old and excite easily when there is something that agrees with my tired jaw and missing teeth. I act fast, for there is little time left for me. You, though, should chew slowly and experience fully what it is that you chew. We were at the darkness."

I have to prove to the old man that I have practiced my movements enough for them to be spontaneous, just as an actor learns his lines so he can speak them naturally. "I creep and look for what the dark will allow me to see," I say. "With those clues alone, I make my way in total silence, in stealth to my victim."

The recliner creaks as the old man rocks in his seat. "And so you creep," he says. "What is on your breath?"

"Banana," I say. "And roast beef and Phillie and pilsner. Not necessarily in that order."

"Is it intrusive, all this odor?"

"The roast beef and the banana remind me that I have eaten, that I have the strength to continue. The beer and cigar remind me that I may take pleasure in my training."

"And the pickle?"

I pause.

The old man looks at me, horrified. "There was a pickle with your roast beef sandwich?"

Yes, there was. That flimsy spear. It looked as nutritious as a jellyfish tentacle. I left it behind in my rush to return to the trailer.

"There was a pickle," the old man says, "and you can't tell me there wasn't. You were offered a pickle and you ignored it! O, O, O!" The old man throws himself back feebly against the recliner. Frank ditches the flailing ship. "Where will you be without the pickle on your breath to remind you of all you have offered to you that you are grateful for?"

I wiggle my toes. I scratch my upper lip. I am that sloppy child again, my bared knife as stealthy as a disco ball. An undisciplined child who spilled blood with no art or wisdom. A child who was plucked up by the nape and pummeled with a ladle by this old man who can barely hold up a banana anymore.

The old man continues, because he is the old man and that alone earns him the privilege. "And now my end is slighted, for you have neglected your pickle! What is left but to start over, wipe it all clean and go back to the beginning? Your art is not to choose correctly among all options at every step but to not make the wrong choices. There is a difference if you chew on that long enough!"

The old man pulls in his lips to give me a chance to reflect. He does not pause long. "You do not learn your art. You do not itemize it like a checklist. You live your restrictions. Next time, you may know this better."

He pockets the ladle and pulls out his Game Boy. As he fits together various shapes into perfect rows, which then dissolve away with celebratory tones, I leave the trailer. The cold is more unforgiving than before. I hear a door on the

Bonneville slam, then the crunch of gravel and dirt as Andre runs towards me. In the dark, I can barely make out his body, but his teeth and eyes seem to run on batteries. With a little training, he could move in the dark like a piece of the night itself.

"Time to pay, whitey," Andre says. "I'm here to make your skinny ass pay."

I rub my hands together for a little warmth. The lights inside the trailer go out.

Writing the Blue Book

This book I'm writing? The cover I have down. The cover will be something to behold. That much is certain.

The cover was my neighbor's idea. My neighbor is assisting me with this book. I lie on his floor, talking talking talking about the book, and he tells me one day, there I am on his floor in mid-thought, "You need a blue cover, man."

"Explain," I say. My eyes go in his direction, though I still can't see him.

"Blue," he says. My neighbor is an artist. He is all set up to start painting me, but he is not up for it yet. He is talking with the end of a brush between his teeth. "Give it a blue cover. Stark raving blue. Blue with no good name for it. Maybe the book's what's it?"

"Title?"

"That. Title. Maybe that towards the bottom, but that's only maybe."

My neighbor the artist hangs his stuff in bookstores. Sometimes his work sells. Other times there are complaints to the management.

Another time he suggests, "Blue binding, too. You need a blue binding. No name, nothing. Save that shit for the inside."

From the floor, I ask, "You know binding, but you don't know title?"

"So I get a day job," my friend says.

The painting my friend is doing now is of something like a fetus—not quite human to be sure—in trouble. Under attack from these strawberries, maybe pomegranates. A spray of dangerous-looking seed. Who knows what this fetus did to get the fruit so irate with it.

So a blue cover it is, a blue binding, blank, to jump out from all those loud bindings, those imitations of font and style from popular books, etc. I can see my book written on the ceiling of my neighbor's loft. I see my neighbor painting lines through it, brush strokes like a blind or crazy editor's pen. Brush strokes very Rorschachian.

When I leave my neighbor's, these words gleam inside my head. They sit there expectantly.

I take coffee before sleep. Relaxes me, actually. The words glow like fluorescent stars on the walls and ceiling of my room, but as I keep my eyes closed, they fade into the dark.

ESSAYS

Violence:
Prince Naseem v. Wayne McCollough
(October 31, 1998)

NOTE: some names have been changed to protect those
who should be more innocent

An evening bred and seeded from violence. Steeped in violence.

The violence began some months before, when my friend Connolly escaped his family life to drop $7,000 and many an alcoholic beverage in Atlantic City. Connolly plays craps hard and fast: $300 on eight, $300 on six, $100 or so on the pass line...you get the idea. He's the 'one more roll' type—one more roll, just one more roll, who knows what fortunes the next roll will bring.

Connolly does not have $7,000 to drop at the craps table. Violence to his assets. Violence to his marriage. Violence to his body—Connolly commands that the waitresses bring him three beers at a time to hold him over until they can bring another three.

Money dropped, money gained, money dropped again, Connolly heads back home to northern New Jersey with a heavy marker to pay. At the Garden State Parkway, he guesses wrong and turns south, towards Cape May, the opposite end of the state. Somewhere near Sea Isle, he discovers his folly. A quick nap, and back he goes.

Oh, the tug that must have been at him when those signs for the Atlantic City Expressway emerged, as did those lights foreboding fortune off to his right...

He was to come back, bringing friends.

Mankind enters first, walking akilter with the affect of a psychotic distracted by his voices. Aluminum fencing reinforced with crossbars encases the wrestling ring. This is not your usual professional wrestling ring cage: it has no open expanse at the top, and it leaves a good three or four foot moat of space around the ring. It is the Cell. The match is Hell in a Cell. It has come to pass once before. That match ended in blood, much blood, and this one only promises more. Mankind is a defamation wrestler: this man has cut himself often for his sport. He is missing part of an ear, left it on a sprig of ring rope for the enjoyment of the fans. His body is a little soft, a little less than sculpted. Frankly, it is broken up to all hell. If all we can say about professional wrestling is that it is fake, then this man has broken his body all for naught, for no one is getting the message.

Connolly scores us a comp suite, dinner and tickets to the Naseem-McCollough fight through The Wild, Wild West, an extension of Bally's Park Place. Connolly and I and our mutual friend CG take dinner in a pseudo-Mexican restaurant that looks more like a Hollywood set than any kind of venue for ethnic fare. One expects banditos with filthy, filthy sombreros to come clinking in, demanding tah-KEE-la, their shoe-polish brown faces scrunched up in constipated glory.

Everything is on the house. We start with tequila and beer, then onto beer and tequila, then a beer with tequila coming later, then straight tequila. We stick with the Dos Equis (which the WASPy waitress in the polyester rebozo calls Dos Equus), but when it comes to the tequila, we work hard to check off every variation on the menu—gold to reposado— but I respond best to the blanco, a liquid clear as water that fries at first contact but then goes down like sugar water after a while (some say that tequila shots get progressively harder to do, but don't you fucking listen to them for a second).

Before each shot, we strike our glasses together and call each other scalawags and ne'er-do-wells, for we are the high rollers tonight who wine and dine on the house. We are the ones duped in with free room and board in hopes that we lose big when we drag our drunk asses to the tables, so who gives a high holy one if anyone else is a little bothered by our raucity? We dump into our receptacles lubrication of the most alcoholic sort. We order dead animals steeped in fattening sauces and moan our approval. Drinking tequila is not enough, for this joint laces everything else with it: the barbecue sauce, the coleslaw, the cheesecake. The cerveza comes in thick, glass mugs that land on the table with a satisfying thump. We are big, ferocious men who have the power tonight, who are in the spotlight, who have a free ticket. We are men doing violence to our bodies and condoning the violence done to the dead animals before us. The staff waits on us happily and reminds us the tip is separate. We are happy, meat-eating men who are glad to gratuitize well the wench who keeps our plates and glasses full.

The Undertaker is one of those awesome wrestling specimens: just under seven feet tall, massive arms enshrouded in painful-looking sleeves of tattoos. Mankind waits for him atop the Cell, and The Undertaker obliges. Mankind of course takes advantage of his climbing opponent and strikes The Undertaker on the side of the head before he can pull himself all the way up. But this is the Hell in a Cell—no one wants an evening of fake strikes accompanied by foot stamps for effect. So the two men soon face each other atop of the Cell, and soon it is The Undertaker with the advantage, and soon it is Mankind in a precarious position: at the edge of the Cell, arena floor looking him in the face.

Then, a move that stuns the crowd entire, even the naysayers that must be out there: The Undertaker flings Mankind forward off the Cell, and Mankind falls twenty feet or so onto a broadcast table. No matting. No buffer beneath the wooden table. The thing gives, but with a crunch that sends shocks through your lumbar and flaps the organs with the blowback. A crew much like the kind that swarms around a stunt double at the tail end of full body burn descends upon Mankind. Mankind assures them he is fine, but while they load him onto an ambulance gurney, he confides to them that the table hurt like a mutherfucker.

Connolly, CG and I get to the Convention Center during the last preliminary. An Irish fighter is going for the title tonight, and the Irish immigrant contingency of the entire Tri-State area must be here. The prelims battle themselves silly, but the Irish want to see Irish, so a brawl has already broken out and the beer stands have closed. Our seats are in a heavy crowd of Irish, who sing and bleat air horns and wave flags and boast rugby shirts.

"We're among the Irish, lad," Connolly tells me in his best brogue.

"Aye, lad," says CG, "the Irish. You got to be Irish too, me boy."

I smile and agree and take manly pats on the shoulder. My name is Seamus now, Seamus O'Weems, and I'm Irish goddamn it. You tell me different, I'll kick your face in.

McCollough enters with not nearly as much presentation as Naseem will. Our seats give a great view down the aisle, and before the McCollough entourage starts their march towards the ring, the Irish's wife hands him their daughter. Daddy's going to get his brains beat in for money, honey. Daddy's going to get his nose broke in four places, and everyone is here to watch him put up a fight, though all the odds say that he is going to lose. McCollough kisses the lass and passes her back.

Naseem enters under Michael Jackson's "Thriller." Echoes of flesh-eating zombies, but pansy-ass dancing ones. The boy can bob and weave like a snake, but who the fuck is here for a boxing match? We Irish want to see someone's clock get cleaned by a good Irish lad. We Irish want blood. We Irish want to see somebody get a good tarring.

*

Yet, the match continues. Before the paramedic crew can roll Mankind out of the arena, the wrestler struggles up from the gurney. His right arm dangles as he makes his way back to the Cell. The fight continues, but there seems no way to surmount the level of violence already attained with the twenty-foot drop. Not another drop from the top of the Cell and through it this time, to the ring, not a leg drop by Mankind onto a chair covering The Undertaker's face.

The Undertaker bleeds from an incision he makes in his forehead while he is supposedly groggy from the leg drop, but we all know this trick. Yeah, yeah, blood, yeah, yeah. We've seen the older wrestlers, they're foreheads a coleslaw of scars from years of slicing themselves with the razor blades they hide in their wrist tape. Yes, we know the actual violence that happens every now and then: we know King Kong Brody got stabbed to death by his own tag team partner in the locker room before their match; we know Killer Kowalski kicked his opponent's cauliflower ear clear off his head and the referee felt it quiver when he picked it up and put it in his pocket; we know the drug ODs (Brian Pillman) and the sudden deaths (Quickdraw Rick McGraw) and those who got so goddamn big their own bodies crushed them to death (O hail Andre, Andre the Giant!). Oh shit do we know how Dr. D David Shulz smacked around that 20/20 reporter and never appeared in the big leagues again. So what are you going to entertain us with NOW?

Mankind knows the game. He hasn't massacred his own flesh all these years for nothing. He's set himself on fire, thrown himself on a bed of nails for crowds in Japan, dropped backwards onto a miniature charge of C4. No way we're getting through this match without a little more self-mutilation.

While The Undertaker lies stunned in the ring, Mankind rolls to the floor and produces a sack of thumbtacks from behind one of the ring posts. A bright, shiny shower of silver as he pours them out onto the ring. He lifts The Undertaker and beats him back toward them, but The Undertaker does not fall. So Mankind jumps onto the Undertaker's back to stun him with a nerve hold, his fingers jammed into The Undertaker's mouth. The Undertaker lifts Mankind onto his back. One step back, then two. Mankind is in the air just above the thumbtacks, riding piggyback.

Then the drop.

Mankind rolls around in the thumbtacks for effect—thumbtacks in his upper arms, in his legs, all up and down his back. There are even some stuck to the back of his head! This match is over! This match is over! The bloodthirsty are a bit shocked, the skeptics aghast that someone would go this far just for an act.

Naseem has danced and woven and hot-dogged for far too long. McCollough has taken the fight to him—this kid is here to bust heads. We Irish have danced jigs up and down the aisles between rounds. We Irish have hooted at every solid punch. We Irish are hitting each other in a common wish to bitch-slap that Prince Naseem and make him cry.

The fight goes all the way to the final bell, despite the experts' best predictions. We Irish *know* who's won, and nothing the 'Let's Get Ready to Rummmmmmmmblllllllllle' guy can say will lead us to believe otherwise.

Two Irish lads next to me, two fine boys who have taken the armrest covers off their father's recliner and wear them on their heads, turn to me just before the decision is read.

"We're going to riot," they tell me, "if our boy doesn't win. Are you going to riot with us, boy?"

Fakir Musafar, the modern primitive, the man anthropologist Charles Gatewood called an "Astronaut of Inner Spaces," had this to say about modern spectator sports (mind you, this as he inserted sticks into his chest to hang from until he spoke to the Great White Spirit or ripped the flesh from his chest): he found the violence in them too outward, too much performed only by a few and watched by the rest. "In our culture, it's all secondhand...they're trying to have a physical life vicariously." Fakir Musafar sees enlightenment in those who have the courage to inflict the suffering upon themselves to rise above the body.

If this is the case, then McCollough and Naseem (well, maybe not Naseem) are high priests of having-their-heads-bust and the budding rioters next to me merely seers of their light. Mankind must be HH the Battling Lama, the bodhisattva of self-infliction, maybe even the White Spirit himself, the entity Fakir Musafar was going to torture himself in honor of, all for the chance for a moment's revelation.

Maybe Fakir Musafar has a point. But still: a riot? I turn to CG and Connolly and tell them, "Riot." I turn back to my Irish brethren with those ridiculous strips of fabric strapped to their heads.

"Yeah," I say. "I'll riot with you."

The Irish boys punch my shoulder in camaraderie. And as soon as their backs are turned, Connolly, CG and I make for the nearest exit. The decision is read, and as we push open the doors, we hear the chant of "Bullshit...bullshit...bullshit..." The promise of some real violence, with cops and billy clubs and contusions and busted capillaries staring us in the face, and we take the back door out. Mankind has a reduced ear to show off his years in the ring, and believe me it is an ugly fucking sight. CG, Connolly and I exit safely onto the Atlantic City boardwalk, living our physical life vicariously...

But, then again, there still awaits a night of other self-injurious behavior. The violence of drink, the violence of gambling...the violence inflicted upon the throat with the sucking of a damn good cigar.

Rules of Combat

NOTE: All quotes and paraphrases re Poetic Terrorism come from the essay of the same name by Hakim Bey (*T.A.Z.: The Temporary Autonomous Zone, Ontological Anarchy, Poetic Terrorism*; Autonomedia, 1991).

Art as crime; crime as art.

I steal from Barnes & Noble. I use my height to my advantage. I lift to-be pilfered book to the top of my head and bounce it against the back of my skull thoughtfully to pass it above the crime detectors (ironic that they're magnetic: in this case opposites do not attract).

Here's a rule: *the best poetic terrorism is against the law, but don't get caught.*

I give back to Barnes & Noble too. When I get pissed at a book for its banality—a Nicholson Baker's *The Fermata* for example, or an Ethan Canin (you choose) or a T.C. Boyle—I tear out pages, tear off halves to staple back together in no discriminate order, make origami, add words in paper-seeping black marker (AMNESTY FOR PIGS or KILROY LEFT US BEHIND ALREADY) but I leave the cover the same, pristine and unread and apparently sellable.

Vandalize only what must be defaced.

These sculptures of graffitized blanderture I then leave on Barnes & Noble bookshelves in proper order. Let someone with some inkling of submitting himself to Barth's *On With the Story* (which convicted itself in my literary trial with its first redundant echoing of Jack's boorish obsession with Scheherezade) be accosted with the realization that he holds in his hand a poetic terrorist object. Poetic terrorism is not done for other artists: *Do it for people who will not realize (at least for a few moments) that what you have done is art.* Let him revile at the heresy and let him be thwarted in his bloated attempt at the literary. Let him pull up allusions to book burning and banning. May he then read a banned book, though I wouldn't dream of suggesting which one.

Poetic terrorism ought to be at least as strong as the emotion of terror—powerful disgust, sexual arousal, superstitious awe, sudden intuitive breakthrough, dada-esque angst...

I may rail against these big-chain bookstores and their crimes of commodified creativity and the promotion of ignorant merchants who can tell you more of what's on sale than what book last left trails of warm grease making parallel lines from the corners of their mouths, yet I spend hours there sucking down chai and scrawling in acid-free sketchbooks (stolen from the bargain table, which makes me feel guilty because who wants to steal that crap anyway?) and getting friendly with the help. I went gaga for the barista who had actually read *The Wrestler's Cruel Study* and Barthelme's *Sixty Stories*. I made sappy advances at her between biscotti. Love always has its own bag of poetic terroristic tricks to fuck your brain. If you haven't been stupid for a literate redhead my friend, don't dross my path unless you're decked in a little riot gear. That, or stay clear of the goddamn coffee shop.

Don't worry. My passion lies not only in destructive force. I made a raid on the local college bookstore when, back in Florida, my professor Marjorie Sandor glumly announced that her book had been remaindered. "Makes a cheap Christmas gift," she said. "At least you can get it signed."

All I needed to hear. Off I went to have at the creature that dared label itself an 'official' bookstore. I lifted up a pile of

Sandors for $2.99 per and let them drop audibly to the counter.

"It's a shame," I declared, "that such a fine writer as Marjorie Sandor should be bought so cheaply." I looked with disdain at the overpriced textbook section. "With all this drivel, you'd think something worth something to this world could earn a modicum of respect" (my dealings with Beckett at the time were definitely affecting my speech).

My point made, I left noisily. Later, as Marjorie dedicated the books to anyone I could think of, Michael, a fellow graduate student, entered empty-handed.

"I just thought you'd want to know," he said, "that I tried to get one of your books, but when I asked at the bookstore why they didn't have any more copies, they said *Richard K. Weems* had come by." Hurricane K. Weems would have been more like it, fucking Tsunami Weems, the store wrecked worse than a trailer park with a bullseye painted on top of every doublewide, the name of their destructor etched onto their hearts, even though I never identified myself and paid only with cash.

Perhaps there is already an FBI file out on me. I gave Michael a copy that was dedicated to Thurgood Marshall—a nice-sounding name. Definitely worth being dedicated to.

My greatest enemy, what stirs me to plan action, is of course what I fear the most—complacency. It is easy to continue with book theft now that I've mastered the technique; easy to tear into books, easy to ridicule authors I've ridiculed before. But to not allow change and appreciation and growth of terroristic techniques and targets is not to admit that the world is empty, malleable and revisionist. The present affects the future. The future affects the past. The past over time becomes more and more different from how we remember it. It is not enough anymore to desecrate the easy targets, never enough to say only nay. Love is as strong a passion as terror, and for all my banter on the banal I can sit and laugh sincerely as Disney's

Hercules plays (without sound) on a video store wall or actually find myself enjoying a story by John Updike.

Still, *not* narrowing down one's field of enemies is always a wise choice, for there are always targets to be had. For the photos taken during an interview with a very stuck-up and WASPy feng shui 'expert,' I'm the guy in the back with his hand on his chin, his middle finger pressed deliberately against his cheek, his eyes also subtly flipping the bird.

Dangerous Theater

In his great book on theater, *The Empty Space*, Peter Brook delineates some different types of theater through their aesthetic philosophies. There is the Deadly Theater (that which fails to recreate itself for its representations and relies merely upon complacence, standardization, or any other lack of creativity), the Holy Theater (that which transcends through any one particular show into something beyond us all), the Rough (vulgar) Theater, and the Immediate Theater (that which asserts itself in the present moment).

There is one type of theater missing from Brook's list: Dangerous Theater. Theater of Danger. The theater that challenges our very assumptions of performance and our part in it, even as spectator, and denies us a safe place to hide.

Then again, how could Brook have not forgotten it? Indeed, the Dangerous Theater pervades his entire book, for how can theater not be dangerous if it revises all we know and lets us leave in one piece only if we agree to accept that we are leaving not entirely as we entered? Deadly Theater is deadly only unto itself. Dangerous Theater, for starters, puts at risk the version of us who was perfectly happy and content to live in this world before having seen what we have seen.

Consider the following example: I lent my friend CG my GWAR concert video. I had told him many a tale of the Scumdogs of the Universe, for I am a big fan. I told him time and time again that, to really know the GWAR experience, nothing matches witnessing live the geysers of blood shooting from the stump of a recently decapitated O.J. Simpson, or the hanging guts of a resurrected Jerry Garcia, or the jism shooting straight and true from lead singer Oderous Urungus's massive, diseased penis.

Still, I had the videotape, bought more for the purpose of spreading the gospel than for my own two-dimensional enjoyment, and he borrowed it. He presented it back to me over a bar, our usual venue for conversation, and said for all to hear, "Weems, never until the moment I popped this video into my VCR did I ever think I led a sheltered life."

Dangerous Theater is a danger to the person you were the moment before you walked into the theater. If you are not willing to let this person go, this theater can be absolutely deadly.

I remember leaving a performance of Blue Man Group, having been bewildered for the previous two hours with a show with no plot, a few characters, and lots of drumming. Let's not forget the super-sized box of Cap'n Crunch, or the Twinkies Lite in the green-striped box. The show itself was an inundation of information, evinced best by the three Blue Men (aptly named, right up to the top of their blue-painted bald wigs) each wearing a red, scrolling marquee, each marquee conveying completely different information, each chastising you for trying to read all three and getting a garbled message rather than trying to get all the information off only one. I came out of the theater happy—the self I was before this show had been released into the ether, the information superhighway if you will, and there was little left to do but lie back on the parked car nearest to me (a shootable offense in New York City!) and tell the gods above, "All right, I can die now. Go ahead. No resistance here."

But of course the truly intriguing thing about Dangerous Theater is that the danger doesn't stop there. Good Dangerous Theater puts everything at risk. C. Carr, writing about the Greenwich Village performance art scene, talks of artists putting themselves in direct lines of danger. Marina

Abramovica and Ulay slithered naked around a stage with an unfed python. They slapped the stage to try to attract its appetite. Chris Burden put himself on display at a gallery strapped to the concrete floor with copper bands. Also on display were two buckets of water with live wires submerged in them. It would have been easy (and in some ways inviting) for any spectator to dump out the buckets and electrocute him.

Even Laurie Anderson's show, "Songs and Tales from Moby Dick," presented its own dangers to those involved. The night I went, Laurie emerged at the very start of the show, her smacked-in-the-back-of-the-head gaze particularly tense, to tell us that the actor playing Ahab was not going to be performing that night, and that his parts would be read by other actors in the company. Since Ahab was one-fourth of the cast, this presented a new challenge for all on stage. Laurie Anderson herself occasionally donned the greatly exaggerated Ahab stovepipe hat. Later I was to find out that Ahab had a bad fall in rehearsal, the orchestra pit his white whale, his peg strained.

Another danger about Laurie Anderson: I have never seen anyone utilize a headset microphone so well in performance. The danger is the loss of theater training, the bellows of 'theater voice,' but for her the danger is legitimate—necessary —for it seems there is no seeing Laurie Anderson without her cast bobbing tiny microphones from just above their ears. Dangerous Theater rethinks every convention and uses only what it must, what it should, what would do best to put all things in most grave danger. And this begs the question: What is theater? Where does the performance lie? Is the theater on the stage, or what's going on in the audience's souls? Is the theater in the concert hall or in the mosh pit in front of the stage? C. Carr talks of performances that have nothing to do with stages, performances geared to audiences of one, performances that were not done before audiences at all: a man and a woman, having never before met, living a year with an eight-foot length of rope between them. They did not invite in audiences to experience their lives. They didn't want an audience at all. Chris Burden had a friend shoot him in the arm in the name of art. When Annie Sprinkle, porn star-turned-performance artist, is in stirrup position with a magnifying scope up her twat, allowing volunteers to come see her cervix, is her offer itself the theatrical event, or does the Dangerous Theater become a real event only when guys and gals get on their hands and knees and get a gander of a piece of genitalia hardly a soul has ever taken a good, serious look at before? I myself had a moment of trying to discover where the actual Theater was in my performance. I was at a party, boasting proudly my Harley-Davidson tee. A nice enough woman asked what kind of Harley I rode. I rode none. She winced and told me my outfit was sacrilege when I knew not the feel of a hog between my legs.

So I told her this story:

I went to see Napalm Death back in the early `90s, back when it was still the original line-up, back when the music purported pure insanity (40-track albums 35 minutes in length, that kind of thing), and it was a rough crowd: bikers, mostly. We're talking the mean type of bikers, the kind who stomp their way through mosh pits brandishing lit cigarettes and chains and spike, the kind with tattoos gracing the whole spans of their backs, the kind who get ornery if you make eye contact. Bikers who get hit hard in the pit and pay back tenfold. Badass biking mutherfuckers.

So the pit was treacherous. No crowd surfing, for surfers probably would have been pulled down and mashed in the head for their effort. Four guys on stage, one behind a flurry of drumsticks, the other three hairy and dirty and oily and just shredding the fuck out of the PA system. A large hog-rider went down in the pit, and social Darwinism ensued—fellow bikers just started kicking the shit out of him.

So I went in. I'm 6'5", over 300 pounds, and I managed to free him from the mudhole stomping. In gratitude, he bought beer and tequila and praised my soul while we pulled at the shirts stuck to our bodies. We shook our hair at each other, the sweat-soaked clumps slapping our heads loudly.

"You're fucking good," he told me. "You hold your own."

"That was not a crowd you want to find yourself on the floor with," I said.

"Yeah, but you're good," he said. It seemed a kind of revelation to him: a four-wheeler, a man who has never licked bugs out from between his teeth, holding his own in a crowd full of his kind. He pulled off his own Harley shirt and pressed it to me.

"You're not supposed to have one of these," he told me, "but fuck them, buddy, you earned it. Anyone gives you shit about it, you tell them you paid for this shirt with blood. You say you fucking bled for this shirt."

And these were the words I repeated to the woman who warned me of my trespasses into hog country. She promptly shut her hole.

So which was the stage where the Theater of Danger gave its dance? Was it the one Napalm Death trod upon? Was it the Harley-laden pit, teeming with violence? Was it the presentation of the Harley shirt to the infidel? Maybe it was in me, clapping the trap on my bitchy party counterpart. But perhaps the stage held us all simultaneously across time. Not one of us came through any of that experience the same way. None of us was allowed to be comfortable with our then-present situation. We all needed to accept a new paradigm of the universe, and it looks as though in each case there was a little blood spilled.

Sitting Danny Rolling

The South is a sea of unsophisticated proteins, northern Florida a regular primordial stew. The heat alone makes one wonder how water-breathers could have seen anything so promising on the nearby beach that they wanted to evolve up onto it. As a New Jersey high school punk, I had been fully indoctrinated into the evils of the South: its Bible-thumpers, snake churches and inbred psychoses. The Dead Kennedys had convinced me of Winnebago warriors and the goons of Hazzard, and hell I was still traumatized by Andy Kaufman getting his neck split open by a Tennessee wrestler. So when I moved to Gainesville in August of 1991 to study fiction writing at the University of Florida, I had my guard up and was ready to fend off any hints of backward southern living. I was a Northern writer who aspired to styles like those of Raymond Carver or Ernest Hemingway. I wrote about sad, beaten-down characters who yearned for something in their lives, but I never knew what that something was, and as a result, neither did they. They were polite stories, full of mystery that never got resolved (or even brought to light)—in other words, uninteresting and unreadable.

I arrived in Gainesville soon after the student murders, but before authorities had a culprit in custody. In essence, I had walked into a herd of wild filet mignon detecting a slight hint of carnivore in the air—but instead of mass hysteria and self-protective rioting or vigilantism, the student body lolled about with a dull foreboding of what they most likely considered their proper place in the world. There wasn't even a sense of avoidance—many students were keeping to their regular routines, as though there was little to be gained from running away from the inevitable. Only faith in a higher order in the universe allows us anxiety and a sense that we have a calling that will be fulfilled barring bad luck. But in Jurassic Gainesville, we were back on the food chain, and a hungry predator was out there, so all we could do was hope that we wouldn't get caught limping by the water hole.

I hung in the folds, too new to the area to chance grazing the fields alone. As a result, my stories turned violent, full of characters who were full of rage, but still I had no sense of the source of that rage, and so whether my characters shot up prairie dogs or forced young girls to be their girlfriends, their actions remained empty and without motive, so I watched the news both for any promise of safety as well as to look for the wellspring for rage in the world. Anything strange got immediate attention from the press, but in Gainesville, Florida it was hard to find something that was *not* strange. This was home of the Grand Poobah (whatever) of the nation's largest chapter of the Ku Klux Klan. This was a land void of manifest destiny, where bugs of the most alien sort pretty much dictated whether you got to finish your box of Kix or had to throw it out and let the larvae grow. This was gator country. Not only had alligators taken hold in every natural body of water in the area, but a local town had a horn they sounded when an indigenous thirteen-foot bull made its monthly round through the town's main drive, the citizens cooped up in their trailers hoping they didn't smell too much like pork rinds. The University of Florida crew team practiced in a creek that had the highest proportion of gators to water in the entire state, effectively reducing the occurrences of the rowers tipping their shells. Gainesville was in easy walking distance of at least four state penitentiaries.

First, the wrong man confessed to the murders after beating up his grandmother. Then, a voice-driven chronic schizophrenic set a rash of church fires. A five-foot lizard was loose in town for a while, eating housepets. When the local media asked the University of Florida animal labs if the lizard was theirs, the labs said they weren't missing any. (These were serious labs—in 1991, UF held the world record for the largest water buffalo born of embryo transplant.) The news held no hope that our stalker in the high grass had either been caught or had moved upwind for something tastier, and we dumb beasts still mulled about as if staying in herds made a difference.

Even when cops caught the real killer, Danny Rolling, the weirdness continued. Alachua County wasn't sure it could afford the trial and applied for state funding. At his arraignment, Danny, a budding country-western singer/songwriter and recently engaged to Sondra London, got up and sang an original composition to his true love in place of a statement in his own defense. The Florida Supreme Court later passed a statute forbidding Danny, his fiancée or his brother from profiting on the book Danny had written about his life and crimes. For this reason alone, knowing that none of the guilty would see a cent from my purchase, did I eventually read it—an awful book, most disappointing in that Danny blamed the murders on a demon named GEMINI. It may take a demonic side to bite off a victim's nipple and take it home with you in a sandwich bag, or saw off a head with a hunting knife and put it on display before you leave a blood-stained bedroom, but don't get cheap and blame everything on temporary memory loss due to demonic possession.

But the killer had indeed been caught, and this gave off miniscule flashes of hope. It was a brief respite back into the Age of Man, for Rolling had been tackled by Greek drama—he had left his hubris dangling.

What had doomed Danny Rolling was his calling to music. While hiding from police, Danny would find a dark area to camp out, build a fire and compose. He sung of rape and brutality and the biting of nipples, and at the end of one tape he did a Johnny Cash and announced himself: "My name is Danny Rolling." This tape eventually got into the hands of police and it was played on the news under a picture of dear, dear love-struck Danny in mid-croon to his Intended in the courtroom. Even the sweetest of grannies would have lobbied to pull the switch herself upon hearing the true face of that monster.

Meanwhile, I was tooling away at stories about men throwing bottles at their estranged wives, about sad people with dark lives, but nothing seemed to be clicking. I ended up throwing away almost every story I had written during my first year in Gainesville. None of my characters inspired any kind of three-dimensional feel. My characters had problems that I thought were the stuff of great stories—love, regret, loss—but their loves and regret and losses never felt real to me nor to anyone who read them. I had no doubts about my desire to write, but I couldn't get in touch with the depth of these emotions.

The killer caught and doomed to fry, the Floridian lemmings loosened their tight circles, and I felt safe to browse and find my own niche of living with the oddities of this antediluvian culture. I ate lunch on campus every day with the Hare Krishnas because I was too poor to afford anything but free grub, and I was getting very good at playing Frisbee, which the Hare Krishnas played quite (ahem) religiously after eating. Because America is great, three southern fundamentalists preached in the same plaza where the Krishnas did their thing, and no one had more right to this public swatch of land than the other. While the fundamentalists told passing students that they were opening the doors to Hell and would not be happy until they dropped their school books and picked up the good book, the Krishnas chanted and sang, and all was diverse in the world.

But when evening news time came, I would flip among the channels for the latest about the Danny Rolling case. I discussed and dissected every detail with my friend Kevin, an Alabama poet, fellow student and general madman. But we didn't discuss details so much as rhapsodize on just how diseased a mutherfucker Danny Rolling was. We shared details of the murders as they were released, reconstructed crime scenes (verbally, of course), but mostly we were trying to figure out why one break-in would result in rape, murder and mutilation while another would end up in rape alone, another in plain burglary. Rolling was a prolific criminal, but there didn't seem to be a steady pattern behind his actions. It's too easy to envision serial killers as these rampaging Rambos, shooting up movie sets on a regular cycle, by the moon or abusive parents' anniversary. But organized serial killers live among the docile with only a modicum of ickiness emanating towards their neighbors and peers, and certainly not enough for anyone to think there's a nearby crawlspace being loaded up with carcasses. Some killers were even considered pillars of their communities, this while they're luring co-eds to horrid fates on the sly. Kevin and I wanted to understand Rolling's compulsions, his desires and essences that made his killing days as much a part of him as putting his right leg into his pants first or preferring pepperoni and black olives on his pizza.

Son of Sam picked a certain phenotype of female to shoot at. Ted Bundy also wanted a certain look to his women. Dahmer wanted men he could control and force to fulfill his fantasies for love zombies and shrines of immortality, and Richard Ramirez did whatever he damn well pleased. Rolling also had some kind of plan, Kevin and I figured, however chaotic. Something made a killing night deadly, and something else kept simple B & E fully satisfying (let's keep that demonic possession shit out of it). Figuring that out seemed to be the essence of everything, and this is what Kevin and I were trying to divine.

We read newspapers and watched TV for all the information our frying brains could hold, but we also worked on our thesis through some major binge drinking. A good, all-out drunk sometimes brought a kind of clarity intellectual discussion couldn't. We were also on a religious mission to get porcelained, inspired by our artistic alcoholic icon, Peter O'Toole. The idea was to go on a good multiple-day drunk, the only sleep taken during blackouts, until SNAP!—total sobriety. The eyes glaze, the skin dews, and everything you need to know is lying there before you wrapped in microwave-safe paper.

That was the hypothesis at least, and we put it to the test at Kevin's apartment during Spring Break. We anticipated moments of mind-numbing revelation and profound deliberation on Danny Rolling's soul. But mostly it was chugging down Kash & Karry brand banana liqueur (the cheapest booze available) and spending long periods on the couch blissfully unaware of our current state of consciousness. If one of us had an intuition, we'd follow it the best we could, but it usually didn't last long before it became drunken babble and we'd resume staring at the far wall, Marlene Deitrich playing on the CD player and the banana liqueur wedged into the cracks between the cushions for easy access.

And then it was towards the end of our third day that Kevin had a flash—maybe not revelation, but certainly inspiration.

"He was right out back here, man," Kevin said, his eyes suddenly bright with a Ginsu edge. "Let's go find it, man, we gotta go find it Weems, right out back, that's where it was."

I knew right from the very start that Kevin was full of shit. We both knew that Rolling would occasionally camp out at random spots in town to elude police, but we had never heard any indication that Rolling had actually camped out behind Kevin's apartment complex. Kevin had woods back there, a good place to camp out, but why would he only make the connection now?

But Kevin was on to something deeper than the facts, and even if he was only in the height of sweet, sticky liqueur delusion, the manic storm behind his glazed eyes was hard to deny. I agreed to go outside with him.

There was a fire pit out there. That much is certain. An amphitheater of three cinder blocks—one for Danny, one for his tape recorder, and the third? GEMINI seat. Bullshit evil spirit seat. That would be the one in the middle.

And that was the one Kevin planted himself at. A kind of calm came over him, a settling in. A mental reclining. The block must not have been too hard, not too soft, not too hot, not too cold. A real baby bear block.

"He was right here, man," Kevin said, his words chopped by incessant giggles. "Right here man, he sat right here, singing his songs, man. Singing his goddamn songs." Kevin was as certain of this as he was certain of his own hair.

And then it hit me. Not quite inspiration, but more of a revelation. As Kevin tried to evoke Rolling energy up through his ass, waving his hands as if he could incite the dead fire before us, I took in a deep breath and had a good look around me.

There were no lights behind Kevin's complex. Gainesville was a dark, featureless cloud that teemed with insect life that I had only seen up north on Creature Double-Feature. Even in the dark, the very air seemed to wriggle with unyielding life. And all this heat. What creative energy! How could you come to this place and *not* transform, de-evolve, and mutate into something base and in visceral contact with the world? And when that sweet, treacherous kind of mutation takes place, what else is there to do about it but throw your primal rage into a creative scream? If you didn't, you were sure to shrivel into a dehydrated yam in this heat. Kevin had his poetry. Me, my stories. Others turned to thumping their bibles or amassing hubcap pyramids outside their trailers. One of my neighbors had constructed an American flag on her front yard out of hundreds of gallon milk jugs filled with red-, white-, or blue-dyed water. This was the secret behind the Southern whoop, that cowboy hoot that's done in seemingly random moments, out the windows of the pick-up or when the bartender brings your new pitcher of Pabst Blue Ribbon. The brain is boiling off those frivolous layers of evolution that fooled us into this crazy idea that we have one up on nature. You are reduced to a soft-boiled egg of vulnerability, waiting to get chomped by the next passing rodent down the pike, so what is there left to do but whoop it up and declare to the heavens that, if you are going to be quashed like a palmetto bug under the heel of a combat boot, you're going to leave one hell of a stain? While Kevin sat Danny Rolling and played air guitar and was maybe even able to conjure up some feeling of what it would be like to be on the lam, a trail of rape and murder strung out behind him like beer cans following newlyweds, I realized I had no clue about that kind of rage, the rage that makes mankind slaughter mankind. But I did understand the need to sing about it afterwards, to write.

In the end, I finished my masters thesis and got my degree. Most of the stories in there were still somewhat lackluster, maybe even plain, but I did learn something fuller about the scarier side of the world. People are an anxious mixture of godliness and monstrosity—often not good enough for the former, and too easily able to live up to the latter, and that became the stuff worth writing about.

Kevin died before he was forty. He choked to death on a roast beef end in front of the convenience store he'd bought it from. No one heard it, but I have no doubt that he let out his own whoop before giving up the ghost. October 25 2006, Danny Rolling finally got his. Strapped down and injected— that sick fuck didn't get in a last concert before his death.

ABOUT THE AUTHOR

Richard Weems is also the author of *Anything He Wants*, finalist for the Eric Hoffer Book Award, and *From Now On, You're Back*. He is a retired teacher living in upstate New York.

More at www.weemsnet.net.